Praise for *The Secret That Is Not a Secret*

"Fiction has always been the homeland of deceit and desire, how we deceive others and conceal ourselves, how we desire others and are desired. In *The Secret That Is Not a Secret*, ten stories keyed to the ten Jewish mystical archetypes, Jay Michaelson brings his knowledge of Kabbalah into contemporary tales of desire and concealment. As one character suggests, 'Religion isn't sublimated sex. Sex is sublimated religion.' Michaelson's achievement in these magical stories is to imagine just how that is so."

—Rodger Kamenetz, author of *The Jew in the Lotus* and
The Missing Jew: Poems 1976–2022

"Jay Michaelson's parable-esque short stories have a sizable dash of Isaac Bashevis Singer and a substantial dash of the queer modern mystic. Immersed in Jewish tradition and folklore, these stories are both learned and sensually detailed, containing humor, eros, magic, and unexpected heartbreak, and opening unexpected windows to our humanness. From tales of table-golems to anti-queer verses that disappear from the Torah, there's reverence here and liberating irreverence, couched in excellent, engaging prose. One of Michaelson's characters names his personal mystical revelations as a 're-enchantment of the earth.' This book offers narratives that re-enchant the body and soul."

—Rabbi Jill Hammer, author of *Return to the Place: The Magic, Meditation, and Mystery of Sefer Yetzirah*

"In Jay Michaelson's heartfelt story collection *The Secret That Is Not a Secret*, characters struggle valiantly and memorably to reconcile the apparent contradictions of the mystical and material realms of existence. Suffused with both probing intellect and deep emotion, these stories invite readers to embark upon a spiritual quest that's refreshingly grounded in the profound realities of our daily lives."

—Aaron Hamburger, author of *Hotel Cuba*

"Jay Michaelson's inventive and daring collection follows lost souls in Israel and New York, desperate for enlightenment. The stories are queer but universal, skeptical but reverent, intellectually rigorous but full of heart—and with sudden, astonishing turns, they reach transcendence. I can't stop thinking about this book!"

—Jonathan Vatner, author of *Carnegie Hill* and *The Bridesmaids' Union*

"This book is mesmerizing and profound. I was already a fan of Jay Michaelson's nonfiction, but this book brings his unique theological and spiritual perspectives alive on an earthy, human level. His characters' lives are sometimes troubled, sometimes angst-filled, but always deeply examined, and in some cases even enlightened. This is a book that will make you think and feel."

—Haviva Ner-David, author of *To Die in Secret* and *Life on the Fringes*

"Sacred and profane, erudite and engaging, queer and questioning, Jay Michaelson's *The Secret That Is Not a Secret* challenges Jewish traditions and imagines its own sort of transcendence. These remarkable stories cleave to God, the flesh, and what it means to live in a world full of hidden secrets."

—Jonathan Papernick, author of *The Ascent of Eli Israel, I Am My Beloveds*, and *Gallery of the Disappeared Men*

"This newest addition to the well of Queer Yiddishkeit warms my heart and mind. Rabbi Michaelson's ten short stories are like a collaboration between queerness, Kabbalah, mysticism, rebellion, and a deeply Queer Judaism. This book might be fiction, but its awe-inspiring messages are real."

—Rabbi Abby C. Stein, author of *Becoming Eve: My Journey from Ultra-Orthodox Rabbi to Transgender Woman*

"Improvisation and transformation mark the midrashic imagination in Jewish religious and literary culture, and the Kabbalistic orientation upon which it is based. Jay Michaelson's *The Secret That Is Not a Secret: Ten Heretical Tales* demonstrates allegiance to this long-standing approach. What makes these stories heretical is their undeniable traditional nature, and what makes them traditional is their incontestable heretical nature. They compel the reader to imagine the connection between the theosophic mysteries of the divine and the psychological-emotional complexities of the mundane, the sacred and the profane, the holy and the erotic. Perhaps this is the esoteric import of the title, for what after all is a secret that is no secret but the most profound secret that can be divulged only to the extent that it is withheld? The fiction artfully woven by Michaelson beckons the reader on the endless journey to uncover what must be recovered."

—Elliot R. Wolfson, Marsha and Jay Glazer Chair of Jewish Studies at University of California, Santa Barbara

"Sylvia Wynter, Jamaican-born essayist, literary critic, and philosopher of Black studies, once said that at the end of the day, all we have is stories. Stories draw a searing line from the mind to the heart, where lofty ideas meet carnal desire. Jay Michelson's *The Secret That Is Not a Secret* tells ten heretical tales—stories in a Wynterean fashion—of desire framed in the ten luminous emanations where the lines separating truth and heresy are blurred and inverted. Michaelson has given us a work that sparkles with light while living in the shadows of the darkness that accompanies all light. It is a gift to all of us who struggle with the sacred while dwelling in spaces where the sacred refuses to go."

—Shaul Magid, Professor of Jewish Studies at Dartmouth College, and author of *Piety and Rebellion: Essays in Hasidism* and *The Necessity of Exile*

Also by Jay Michaelson

*God in Your Body: Kabbalah, Mindfulness, and Embodied
Spiritual Practice*

Everything is God: The Radical Path of Nondual Judaism

Another Word for Sky: Poems

God vs. Gay? The Religious Case for Equality

*Evolving Dharma: Meditation, Buddhism, and the Next Generation of
Enlightenment*

The Gate of Tears: Sadness and the Spiritual Path

is: heretical blessings and poems (as Yaakov Moshe)

Enlightenment by Trial and Error

The Heresy of Jacob Frank: From Jewish Messianism to Esoteric Myth

THE SECRET
THAT IS NOT
A SECRET

ten heretical tales

JAY   MICHAELSON

Ayin Press
Brooklyn, NY

The Secret That Is Not a Secret: Ten Heretical Tales

This book was made possible through the generous support of the Opaline Fund and Anne Germanacos / Firehouse Fund. We are grateful for their commitment to the transformative power of creative work, and to amplifying a polyphony of voices from within and beyond the Jewish world.

Cover design, book design, and typesetting by
David Benarroch

First Edition
First Printing

Ayin Press
Brooklyn, New York
www.ayinpress.org
info@ayinpress.org

Distributed by Publishers Group West, an Ingram Brand

ISBN (paperback): 979-8-9867803-9-9
ISBN (e-book): 978-1-961814-90-5

Library of Congress Control Number: 2023911505

Ayin Press books may be purchased at a discounted rate by book clubs, synagogues, and other institutions buying in bulk. For more information, please email info@ayinpress.org.

Follow us on Facebook, Instagram, or Twitter @AyinPress.

The Secret That Is Not a Secret

The laws of forbidden relations may not be expounded before three persons; the workings of creation before two; nor the workings of the Divine Chariot before one.

—Mishnah Hagigah 2:1

This may be compared to a man who dwelled among the cliffs and did not know of those dwelling in the town. He sowed wheat and ate it raw. One day he went into town and was offered good bread. The man asked, "What is this for?" They replied, "It's bread, to eat!" He tasted it and asked, "And what is it made of?" They replied, "wheat." Afterwards they brought him cakes kneaded with oil. He tasted them and asked, "And what are these made of?" They replied, "wheat!" Later they brought him royal pastry kneaded with honey and oil. He asked, "And what are these made of?" They replied, "wheat!" He said, "Surely I am the lord of all these, since I eat the essence of all of them!" Because of this, he knew nothing of the delights of the world, which were lost to him. So it is with one who grasps the principle but is unaware of all those delectable delights deriving and diverging from that principle.

—Zohar 2:176a–b (translated by Daniel C. Matt)

THE BEARD

Sara Duberman loathed her husband's beard. She could not abide it; hated to brush up against it in moments of intimacy; could barely stand to look at it, with the crumbs that lodged in its black curls after every meal, or the bits of lint that would cleave to it by the end of every day.

Sara cherished her husband Yakov, who, she knew, had been her soulmate since before they were born, and who had been her husband from the beginning of their long journey back to the ways of God and Torah. Yakov was dear. But the beard was a parasite, affixed to his face like a choking, tangled vine.

When they made love, Sara had learned to contort her head as if in the throes of ecstasy so as to avoid the beard's web. Yakov was a considerate lover, although there were times when Sara wondered whether he was motivated by desire or by the religious duty to please one's wife; when he would touch her in a new way, as he often did, even after thirteen years of marriage, Sara would wonder whether this had been some tip shared at one of his late-night study sessions, to better fulfill a *mitzvah*. But whatever the origin of Yakov's ministrations, he would kiss her, nuzzle up against

mitzvah – commandment

her, and, just a moment before climax, gather her up in his arms and embrace her with the love of the Holy One for his Bride. And when Sara looked into his eyes, her lust fused with his and with the joining of the supernal powers.

But the beard ruined everything. Yakov would kiss her, and the beard would follow, creeping over her belly, tangling itself in her pubic hair. Yakov would lick her right breast, and the beard would tickle her belly. No matter how she twisted herself to get away from it, the beard found her, crept along her like a spider. Occasionally Sara would imagine creatures that lived in the beard, lice or mites or tiny insects, jumping from it to her—into her, she imagined—violating and polluting her, even as her husband tended to her with devotion.

There was no question of Yakov shaving, or even trimming, his beard, and Sara would never ask him to do so. Sara and Yakov were *ba'alei tshuva*: they had grown up in the secular world but were now devout Chabad Hasidim, with pictures of the Rebbe in every room (save the bathrooms) and books full of customs and practices governing every aspect of life. And the beard was essential to a Hasid. Indeed, a few weeks after Yakov first asked Sara whether something was wrong and Sara had answered too quickly, she mentioned casually, in the cramped kitchen, piles of dishes from Shabbos dinner waiting to be washed, that Mendel Gutstein had trimmed his beard short.

"I know. He looks like half a man, doesn't he?" Yakov replied, leaning against the counter.

Chabad – the Lubavitch sect of Hasidim

When they were younger, living under different names in a world with endless freedom and no values, a beard would have been merely a matter of personal choice. Like everything else! But the Jewish life of devotion and purpose is what had drawn them together in the first place, when they each began exploring the religious life. Now, their actions mattered; they were connected to Hashem and His plan for human beings; they were part of a community. Yakov could not be smooth, like his namesake. It was an impossibility.

Sara couldn't remember when the beard first began to trouble her. When they married, it was still relatively short, and besides, they were in the flush of love; all was new, and they were infused with passion for one another and for God. But Dov Baer, their eldest, was now twelve, soon to become bar mitzvah; those days were a long time ago. Now, during the long days while she tended to their house and four children, Sara found herself daydreaming of outrageous circumstances that would save her from the predicament of the beard. She imagined some sort of fire that would singe the beard just enough to trim it—just an inch or two off, Sara thought, would be enough for her to recover the passion she had, years ago, held for Yakov. Sara even found herself musing over what would happen if Yakov fell ill with cancer—nothing that would spread, just enough to justify chemotherapy—until she reproached herself for even thinking such a horrible thing.

Lying in bed late one Friday night, their four children asleep and the *zmiros* from nearby apartments having finally

zmiros – songs

quieted down, Yakov turned to Sara and, instead of beginning the usual acts of lovemaking, asked her, almost in a whisper: "Sara, is everything all right?"

"Of course, Yakov," she answered—too quickly, she thought with a pang of regret. In the secular world, psychological explanations were often attributed to actions and words. Did her rushed assurance in fact suggest the opposite? Did Yakov *know*? But maybe Yakov didn't know, because quickly he seemed to redouble his efforts, kissing her more and more passionately, the beard sweeping along behind him like fraying threads of wool. Sara could not help but recoil, even as she held herself and her stubbornness in contempt. Why could she not make peace with this one little problem, this one flaw? Yet her shudders of revulsion were involuntary; before she realized what she had done, it had been done, as if not by her but by some unseen entity that possessed her. And now Yakov knew that something was wrong, because Yakov was considerate, attentive.

But nothing came of it. The weeks passed. Yakov and Sara were busy; the little one was sick, then Dov Baer; Yakov didn't inquire further into what might be bothering his wife. Yet Sara's despair seemed to grow on her like a vine. She could not confide in her friends; they were all gossips. If she confessed, soon her preposterous little aversion would be the hushed, giggling talk of the entire community. Notwithstanding all the reprobation of "evil speech" and those who engage in it, all of her friends talked ceaselessly behind one another's backs, weaving webs of secrets to the point where everyone knew everything and told everyone except the person or persons involved. So Sara remained silent, letting herself mention the beard only to Dov Baer, whom she loved, and even then only in jokes about the bird's nest on Tati's face. But Sara felt she had to talk to someone, if only to say the words out loud, to give shape to this dread. And so, after much reluctance, she decided to call an anonymous counseling line. All the Hasidic communities had these lines, although no one ever spoke of them. They knew, but claimed not to know, that there were women in their community who had problems with abusive husbands, or with drinking, or with depression. The helplines were a kind of underworld, an open secret, as well as an admission that one could not carry the burden, as was, of course, the Jewish way. At first, Sara stared at the phone but could not bring herself to dial. Several times, as soon as the rings began, she ended the call—twice after someone had picked up. At last, she mustered the courage to stay on the line and explain her situation. The response was dismissive. "Don't think only of yourself," the 'specialist' said. "Remember how important the *minhagim* are to distinguish us from the *goyim* and from the *yiddin* who act like goyim. You should count your blessings! To have such a wonderful husband who provides for you, and cares for you. To have your wonderful children. Stop focusing only on the negative! Be thankful to Hashem for what He has given you."

Sara hadn't expected support and acceptance; this was the path of the secular psychiatrists, whose easy affirmations of sin and imperfection were part of the world she had left

minhagim – customs

behind when she joined Chabad at the age of nineteen. But she had hoped for *something*. A cure, or an answer, or maybe some sympathy—anything to help remedy the situation into which she had fallen. Instead, nothing. "Thank you for the advice," Sara said, stifling her feelings as she hung up the phone.

It was true that Sara's life was an enviable one. Yakov made good money in electronics; her three sons were all healthy and bright boys, and little Ruchel was kind. They had a good home, they participated in the community and its endeavors—could she not bear this one burden?

She could not. Some weeks, she was able to focus on Hashem during sex with Yakov, to think of the unity in the upper realms being brought about through their unity in this one. By losing herself in the spiritual meaning of their sexuality, Sara could, on rare occasions, forget the gross carnality of Yakov and his beard. Yakov was handsome, Sara remembered; you only had to look at Dov Baer to remember how beautiful his father was, underneath the beard, and so she would focus on her memory of Yakov rather than his present reality. Other times, she berated herself—"Think, Sara, of all the *bruchos* that Hashem has given us, focus on them!"—and was able to tolerate the beard out of shame. One time she even forced herself to stroke it, caress it, as a form of punishment. But it was of no lasting use. Sara began to feel as if she were getting lost inside the beard's curly black hairs, slowly, gradually, steadily becoming unable to breathe.

bruchos – blessings

Having failed to accommodate herself to the beard, Sara began to imagine various stratagems that could somehow defeat it. Hair removal powders, or creams—Sara had heard of such things, and these might work, but how to put them on? Could she apply them in his sleep? Only if he was sound asleep—she would need sleeping pills for that. So, sleeping pills in his dessert, the cream while he slept. But wouldn't he smell the lotion when he awoke? Surely he would. And what would happen next? Would he simply accept the loss of his beard as a random occurrence? Surely Yakov would see a doctor, surely he would be concerned. And then the truth would come out. Or, if not medicine, maybe some sort of foul liquid somehow spilled into the beard, forcing Yakov to shave it off—it would be only for a little while, but maybe that short break would be enough. But what then?

It was not the deceit that gave Sara pause. In fact, Sara had long been deceiving her husband—and with his silent consent, she thought. Of their unusually small family—only four children across thirteen years of marriage, and none within the last six—Sara and Yakov had told everyone that this was God's will, and had always said that they felt blessed enough by the children they cherished. But Sara knew that it was not God's will but her secret stash of pills, obtained from a goyishe pharmacist with money Sara had squirreled away. She believed that Yakov knew, had known for years, had to have known. Like Sara, he had experimented sexually in high school before becoming ba'al tshuva; he knew what contraception was. And he never asked after her health, never suggested that either of them should see a doctor about the sudden infertility that had seemed to attack one of them (or both?) in the prime of life. Only silence prevailed. A silence indicating assent.

The only time Sara's deception was nearly exposed was during the ritual search for leaven on the eve of Passover, when Dov Baer, then around ten years of age, stumbled upon Sara's hiding place, held aloft the pills in their distinctive little wheel, and asked, "Is this *chametz*?" Sara grabbed the pills from him and mumbled something about cramps. Fortunately Yakov was in another room at the time. Or perhaps he had heard but preferred it this way; Sara never asked.

And now, Sara devised similar schemes to cope with her current dilemma. One night, Sara lied to Yakov about her menstrual cycle, so as to prolong the period of separation when it was forbidden to sleep together. Another, she tried pleasuring Yakov with her mouth, so as to keep his head and beard as far away as possible, but as she feared, Yakov demurred; as the halacha required, every drop of his sperm would land in her artificially barren womb. She even tried to kiss Yakov less, until he remarked that she kissed her eldest son more than she kissed her husband.

One Friday afternoon, Sara was cooking the cholent on the hot stove, when suddenly she thought: perhaps the counselor, in her misguided way, had a point. What was it, really, that so disturbed her about the beard? There was a reason,

chametz – food prohibited on Passover
halacha – Jewish law
cholent – stew served on the Sabbath

was there not, why this aversion persisted? There had to be. Not some superficial account of her "psychology," but the true root of the distaste. After all, Sara almost said aloud, if we can understand the root of a problem, maybe it can stop being a problem.

Sara knew that everything in the world—Yakov, the beard, her own psychology—was but a shell atop the Divine potencies that order the universe. And since the beard was a manifestation of those forces, the only way to understand it, and thus to overcome her resistance to it, lay in understanding its true meaning, its secret meaning. That would be the answer: the essence of the beard, and her hatred of it, resided not in some simplistic psychological symbolism or physical revulsion but in the hidden secrets of the Divine realms. After all, it had been this mystical aspect of Chabad that led Sara to embrace it fifteen years ago, as a curious college student spending a summer in Israel. Growing up as a Reform Jew, she had never understood the purpose of *kashrus*, or Shabbos, or any of the mitzvos that she assumed only the faithful performed, until a Chabad rebbetzin explained how in our every act we have the opportunity to uplift sparks of holiness trapped in the husks of materiality and to bring about redemption. Behind every act there lay a wealth of hidden, mystical meanings, correspondences in the Divine realms. Decipher the codes, and you could understand the functioning of the universe.

So Sara set out on her quest. She knew from experience that the internet would be useless: the Chabad and other *frum* sites only touched the surface of the matter, and others

kashrus – Jewish dietary laws

were utterly unreliable, full of confusion and error. The answer she sought would be found only in books. So when Yakov was at work, the boys were at school, and Ruchel was playing at a friend's house, she searched her husband's prized bookshelves, careful to replace each volume exactly in its place. She scoured every volume for the slightest hint as to the meaning of the beard. She searched in the books of customs, the Bible, everywhere. But Yakov was no *mekubbal;* he had only the standard Chabad library of Talmud, *Tanakh*, and *Tanya*, with volumes of conversations and letters of the Rebbe. These books did not provide the answers Sara sought. They had only the most rudimentary explanations—one must keep a beard at such and such length, it is a sign of faith, and so on—but said nothing of the hidden, deeper meanings. Sara felt ashamed of her husband's level of learning, that he should be content with such superficiality. Yakov, who as a student had been such an avid reader, suddenly seemed like one content with the surface and no longer thirsty for depth. After several attempts at furtive but thorough searching, Sara gave up. She knew the answers were written somewhere, but they were not on Yakov's bookshelf.

So, at last, Sara resolved to ask a *rov*. It was dangerous; in her community, everybody knew everybody. Sara knew all the rabbis' wives; she knew Hinde, who was having trouble

mekubbal – Kabbalist
Tanakh – Bible
Tanya – central text of Chabad Hasidism
rov – rabbi

conceiving; she knew Frayde, who worked in the library of the girls' school. Still, it was understood that a one-on-one conversation was sacred, confidential—and Sara felt she had no alternative. She contacted one of the rabbis who had helped bring her to Jewish observance, Rabbi Moishe Lander, who agreed to meet with her. And so on a crisp autumn day when the chores had been done and the house was clean, she went in for her meeting. After exchanging pleasantries with the rebbetzin, she entered the rabbi's study, which was cluttered with books and papers. Sara perched on the edge of her chair as if not to disturb anything, and told him her request.

"The mystical significance of a beard?" Rav Moishe asked incredulously, after Sara had posed her carefully rehearsed question. "Why do you want to know of such things? Are you planning on growing one?" Rav Moishe had a grin on his face, but Sara couldn't determine whether condemnation might lie beneath the levity.

"No, rebbe," she replied earnestly. "But it is something that has always made me very curious. I thought that by understanding this, I could understand my husband on a deeper level, that his beauty would be to me more than just his appearance, but something, I don't know . . . higher than that."

"It's a noble wish," the rabbi said, already dismissive, and stroking his own gray-white beard as he spoke. "I think you and Yakov should discuss whether it's appropriate for me to enter into it with you alone. It's not something where I can just give you a simple answer, now, and you can understand.

The meaning of a Jew's beard is tied to some of the deepest secrets of the Kabbalah."

"Well, I don't pretend to have any knowledge of these secrets," Sara said, sitting back a bit more in her chair. "But is there anything, even a *remez*, you could give me? I hate to trouble Yakov with my little curiosities."

"A remez . . . well . . . I can tell you a story, that I heard from the Rebbe himself, on a recording made many years ago. It seems there was once a Hasid who in his business had all the time to deal with the goyim. He was a salesman, this Hasid, and the product he had was very expensive and much beloved by the goyim. He would go—this is in Europe, before the *churban*—he would go from town to town with this product, and sell it in the goyishe markets to their retailers and consumers alike. Everyone liked this product that the yid sold. Now, it was dangerous, what this Jew was doing, because life at that time was not good for the Jews. It's one thing you go and sell from Jew to Jew, going to towns where there's always a *kehilla* and you're protected from the evil of the *klippos*. But this one yid was straying far from where there were any other frum Jews, into the cities where the *maskilim* had perverted the souls of the Jews with their modern ideas and Greek philosophy, and where only a few years after this story takes place, God would punish us all for straying in this way from the Torah.

remez – hint or allusion
churban – Holocaust
kehilla – community
klippos – the "shells" or realms of evil
maskilim – modernizing Jews

"What you have to understand, what I'm sure you do understand, Sara, is that any kind of sickness or tragedy that befalls us, this is God's will, this comes from God. Fortunately for us, this aspect of God's *din* is mediated by *rachamim*; God pities us because we are weak and pathetic, and He doesn't take out His anger on us the way really we deserve.

"Now, you might ask, what does this have to do with your question, with the beard? It turns out that this Hasid thought his beard, which was long and unruly the way sometimes a beard can be, he thought this beard was hurting his business. You know, commercially speaking, it's one thing for the goyim to see a yid and they know he's a yid, but his products are good so they buy. But, thought this poor soul, it's another thing for me to come in a full set of *chassidishe* clothes and a hat and a beard—it's hurting my business. They see me, they turn away. So this little yid replaced his hat with a yarmulke only, the way many of the less frum yiddin do, and he trimmed his beard to be neat and orderly like those of the goyim and the maskilim and people of that sort.

"It turns out the Hasid was right: his business doubled overnight. Where before he had always to get over a certain barrier with his customers, to get past the physical signs that made him distinct, as a Jew should be, from the people around him—now he blended in better. Now, the goyim and the maskilim looked at him, and sure, they saw that he was a yid, but they thought, well, he's someone we can deal with. And the sales of his product increased, as I said, double.

din – judgment
rachamim – compassion

In fact, sales increased so much and his reputation grew so large, that the authorities got wind of this yid who is traveling from town to town and selling this wonderful product and yet not paying any taxes to the government. Of course, by law he wasn't required, but this didn't interest the goyim. No, the goyim fined him for tax evasion, they threw him in jail like the Alter Rebbe himself, and while the yid was in jail—with no one to bail him out, because he was far from any kind of Torah community, surrounded by the forces of evil and the klippos—while he was in jail, some robbers stole all his inventory. He was left with nothing.

"So you see, Sara, it isn't as simple a matter as the Hasid thought. He thought that removing this barrier between himself and the goyim would improve his business, but he didn't think what would happen if his business improved. When we take away the protection that the *kadosh boruch hu* grants us from the forces of evil and the judgments against us, we are on our own, we are exposed—like the face of a man without a beard. We are *mamesh* completely defenseless, and vulnerable. This is a remez of the power of a Hasid's beard."

Sara thanked the rabbi and took her leave, followed by more joyful small talk with the rebbetzin, as if everything were normal and nothing had been revealed. But inwardly, Sara felt her heart quicken. This was a start. It was indeed only a hint, a simpleton's story about protection from evil. But it reminded Sara of when she was younger, as she was

kadosh boruch hu – God (lit. "the Holy One, Blessed be He")
mamesh – really

just beginning to explore becoming frum, when she had read avidly the expositions of the mystical Godhead and the Messiah, of the meanings of the *sefirot*, and of the elevation of the sparks. This was a beginning.

It was Dov Baer to whom Sara finally turned to help her find the answers she desired. Dov Baer was almost a man now, already practicing for his bar mitzvah in long hours of chanting and memorization. It was Dov Baer who had found the pills that Passover eve, like some perverse *afikomen* hidden deep in a drawer. And it was Dov Baer to whom Sara had always confessed her frustrations and dreams, even when he was a little boy and could scarcely understand the words she was saying. Now that Dov Baer was becoming a man, he could be trusted to keep her secret.

Indeed, it seemed to Sara that Dov Baer was becoming a man all too quickly: a thin peach fuzz had begun to appear above his lips, the first visible (to her) inkling of adulthood. Soon the fuzz would darken, and he would grow one of those wispy half beards the teenagers all had, as if displaying to the world the progress of puberty. And eventually, like an inevitable rolling in of the tide, his beard would mature into a bramble such as Yakov's. But this was in the future. For now, he was still Dov Baer, still her dearest.

"Dov Baer, I want to ask you a favor, between just the two of us," Sara said late one night, as she tucked him into bed. The child caught on immediately, and a conspiratorial air filled the room he shared with his sleeping younger brothers.

sefirot – emanations of God
afikomen – portion of Passover matzo

"Okay," Dov Baer said, his voice not yet able to crack in nervousness.

"You know how all Hasidim have beards like Tati's, and how they can trim them but never cut them completely."

"Yes, Mami."

"So you know, of course, that part of the reason for this is to distinguish us from the goyim, who are as a general rule clean-shaven."

"And the halacha not to shave the sides of your head—"

"On the *pshat* level, yes. But what you might not know is that a Hasid's beard is much more than that. It has, Dov Baer, significances that extend beyond this realm into the higher realms. I am telling you this because you too, one day, will grow a beard—and I want you to know its true meaning, its true importance. Dov Baer, I have a reason I cannot tell you for asking you this favor. I want you to trust me. I want you to find for me a *maimar* or a *sefer* or anything at all that discusses the secret meaning and purpose of the beard. Do you understand? This is a personal request. I want to surprise Tati with it, so I don't want you to tell him. Just ask one of your teachers where to look, say it's for your own interest, and bring me the book. Would you do that for me?"

"It's not *ussur* for me to read this book?"

"No. I already spoke to a rov about it. The fact is I could do it myself, but I don't have access to the library like you

pshat – surface, literal meaning
maimar – recorded rabbinic statement
sefer – book
ussur – forbidden

have at school. I'm not looking for a book that's not already readily accessible. If mamesh it's something that we're not supposed to know, then they won't let you take the book out. If they let you take the book out, that means it's okay for anyone to know about. Right?"

"Okay," Dov Baer said, looking up at her.

"Okay?"

"Okay."

"Give Mami a hug." And Dov Baer smiled and rose in bed to embrace her, and she came to him and kissed him lightly near his lips.

The next day, Dov Baer volunteered to help with the dishes after dinner so he could have a moment to speak with his mother. Unwise, Sara thought: such an act arouses suspicion. But Yakov seemed not to notice.

"I checked at school," Dov Baer said over the washing. "I didn't find anything about . . . the topic. But I'll look tomorrow in a different place. I think I'll have success."

And sure enough, two days later, Dov Baer returned with the treasure: a collection of Hasidic teachings on all the different parts of the body, from the head to the toes, and—to Sara's displeasure, receiving this book from her young son—everything in between. "Where did you get this book?" she asked.

"I found it," Dov Baer said. He really was smart, no? Sara thought. Say no more than you need to say. Keep your secrets to yourself, and they remain secrets.

"Thank you, Dov Baer," Sara said, and gave him a kiss on the forehead. "You've made Tati and me very happy."

Sara was elated. She had told herself that she would wait and read the book at a safe time, in the middle of the day, when Yakov was out. But she could not restrain herself. She stayed awake until she heard Yakov lightly snoring in bed. Yakov was a light sleeper, but she would be stealthy. Sara tiptoed out to the living room, taking with her Dov Baer's secret book, and also a book of "advice for women" in case Yakov awakened and asked what she was doing.

What the book told her she could only half understand. It referred to realms of the Kabbalah that Sara had only vaguely heard about, years earlier: the interaction of the different faces, or *partzufim*, of the Godhead, as explained by the Holy Ari. God, according to these teachings, has within Himself an entire family of personalities: a mother and a father; a rambunctious child known as *Ze'er Anpin* (the "short face") containing most of the attributes of God as generally understood; and a bride of the child, the *Nukba*, the feminine presence of God as felt on the Sabbath eve. Presiding over all of them is the *Arikh Anpin*, literally—Sara read with a gasp—the long-faced, or long-bearded, one. This is the Ancient of Days, who mercifully, lovingly presides over the universe and the Godhead itself. Sara read that according to one of the Ari's most important disciples, the beard of the Ancient of Days was no metaphor, but was, insofar as we may speak of such things, a reality. It had thirteen points, each corresponding to an attribute of Divine Mercy, each with its own personality, as it were, and with a special relationship to the soul of every Jew. God's beard was no mere symbol, but was the embodiment of mercy itself, and a man's beard, arrayed in a sort of reciprocal relationship to it, was both an imitation of the Divine and a mechanism for receiving its influx. Sara paused. It was as if Yakov's and God's beards were locked in an unbroken, everlasting kiss.

Hair, Sara continued, ordinarily signifies the aspect of judgment. But just as a long beard becomes soft and pliable, so too the beard of the Ancient Long-Suffering Holy One softens harsh judgments and turns them into mercy for Israel. The bearded face of the Ancient of Days is an expression of the malleability of judgment, an embodiment of the changeable nature of justice into mercy. Now Sara saw that what the rabbi had hinted at in his homily—the protection afforded by the Jew's beard—was not as she had understood it. She had thought the story to be a simple tale about obedience and reward. But no, the beard itself possessed power; in shaving his beard, the merchant was like Samson cutting his hair. The protection, the envelope of rachamim that went with him wherever he went, was suddenly removed. And he was exposed to the judgment he deserved, untempered by the forgiveness he was now unable to receive. To shave one's beard was not only an act of rebelliousness and assimilation—it was vandalism against the antenna attuned to God's mercy. Far from being an alien parasite, the beard shaped Yakov into the form of the kadosh boruch hu, turned him into a sort of mirror of the Divine face. Sara felt a warmth creep over her body, a feeling she had not experienced since the early years with Yakov, learning the mysteries of Kabbalah: the *shefa*, she thought, the divine flow.

It was getting late, but Sara was too inspired to sleep, so she read further Hasidic teachings about the beard and its meanings. She read how Rabbi Nachman relates the "upper beard"' to the "lower beard," and teaches that just as the "lower beard" grows prior to the upper one—Sara paused for a moment to consider her Dov Baer, whose face she had already observed to be slowly turning into that of a man— so too must a man master his lower evil inclination before he is able to merit the revelation of God's higher attributes of mercy. She read how the Rebbe taught that the beard embodies the honor of the man and the transformation of carnality into spirit. She read and read.

The next night was Shabbos, and Sara had just ended the two-week period of separation from Yakov ordained by the laws of *niddah*; it was a time for *yichud*, of union both spiritual and sexual. Lately these times had filled Sara with dread of the beard, but this time, she felt inspired—transformed. As Yakov began his playful ministrations, Sara meditated on the aspects of Divine mercy, on the long-suffering compassionate God who was mirrored in the beard tickling her face. She tried to rise beyond this physical act, to elevate her mind to the symbolic realms, and in so doing move her heart from discomfort to the joy of caressing a symbol of God's love. It was beautiful—for a time.

But the physical remained ineluctable. Even as she turned her mind to the symbolic, spiritual meanings of the beard, the body remained ardently, defiantly corporeal, and its materiality continually interrupted her. There was no

niddah – laws of menstruation

escaping the distraction of the real. Indeed, far from ending
her disgust at the abrasive tentacles of Yakov's facial hair, the
teachings of the Kabbalah had only amplified the disjunction
between the world of the sefirot and the physical world that
she inhabited. A distant, supernal, abstract, metaphorical
beard was an eloquent concept, but the one that tickled her
navel when Yakov kissed her neck remained close, carnal,
repulsive. And the Rebbe? Well, the Rebbe never had to kiss
a beard. He looked on his wife, and her smooth skin, and
her delicate facial bones shaped into a sweet smile. Would
he have praised the "honor" of the beard if he had to spit
pieces of one out every time he made love? It was easy for
him: he simply didn't shave, and received the Godly influx.
But where was the mercy for his wife, her absolution and
forgiveness?

As quickly as Dov Baer's book had lifted Sara's spirits,
now they fell to the earth. Her soul grew dark. On the one
hand, she felt ashamed. Had her relationship with Hashem
grown so cold that she could not endure even a small
displeasure in His service? Sara had gone without some of
her favorite foods for years, had abandoned the prospects of
a career, had cut her hair short and worn a wig to conceal
it—all for the love of Hashem. But on the other hand, what
had she received in return? Sara remembered a time when
she could feel her love reciprocated by Hashem, radiating
from every trembling leaf on every tree. The world, then,
seemed alight with a fiery courtship between her soul and
God's. But now? She had gone to so much effort, had gained
the secret she had sought—so where was God? Where was

her recompense? Sara found herself alienated from the kingdom of heaven and mocking the secrets themselves.

The change did not pass unnoticed. Yakov, already alerted to something being amiss, now grew concerned. Ruchel noticed that Mami didn't offer to play with her as she used to. Itzie and Zalman cried more than usual. But Dov Baer was the worst. He would stare at Sara for minutes at a time, during meals, during Shabbos preparations, glowering at her, as if knowing. He had accepted the book back from Sara and returned it to its source without speaking a word to anyone. But now—this distance. Sara imagined that he knew her torments, in a way that Yakov never could. Dov Baer never cried—he was the eldest—so instead he grew cold and distant. Where was divine mercy now?

One afternoon, as Sara was folding the clean laundry, neatly creasing a set of Yakov's yellowed tzitzis, a flash of realization went off in her mind: The answer! Sara's schemes had always been about somehow changing Yakov; but to escape the beard, she now realized, *she* would have to change. Not spiritually, psychologically, or emotionally— those transformations had already failed—but physically. Yakov had his beard to protect himself from the dinim and attract the Divine mercy, but Sara now needed one of her own—not a beard of hair, of course, but some other form of protection, something that would keep her safe from outside forces, and, at the same time, attuned to Hashem. It would simply be the reverse of Yakov's, the other side of his counte- nance. She could use something like detergent, she thought, looking at the blue plastic bottle in front of her, to create a rash, or an allergic reaction. She would see a dermatologist, who would not know what to make of it. She would remark that the reaction seemed to be in just the places where Yakov's beard had touched her—a mirror-beard, almost, of his own—and the doctor would, naturally, conjecture that perhaps the beard was the cause of the rash. (Perhaps there were other causes, Sara imagined him saying, but the beard could not be ruled out.) And then matters could take their own course. Yakov would not have to shave; he could just leave her alone. For the sake of health, and so permitted by halacha! And anyway, Sara thought, if he would just keep his "upper beard" away from me, his "lower beard" could still play wherever it liked. And so, standing there by the washing machine, Sara settled on a certain cleanser that she had once spilled on her hand while scrubbing the kitchen counters for Pesach, and that had produced a painless but unsightly rash. With a cotton ball, she dabbed the cleanser on her cheeks, the area below her neck where Yakov's beard frequently brushed, even a tiny bit on her stomach. She felt the Divine protection immediately take hold.

Over the next few days, Sara developed a routine for herself: twice daily she would reapply the cleanser until the rash developed. And so it did. Within two days of Sara's routine, a faint irritation had turned to pimples, and then gradually to a rash covering most of her lower face, as well as a bit of redness on the top of her chest. It stung a bit, but nothing Sara couldn't bear. Yakov became alarmed. "What could it be?" he asked one night.

"I have no idea," answered Sara, feigning the onset of

tears.

"You need to see a doctor. Are you putting something on it?"

"I'm putting on lotion, but it doesn't seem to help." Technically, barely a lie.

"Well, you should see someone, a specialist, tomorrow. Tell him it's an emergency. It *is* an emergency."

"I will."

"Please. Sara, I hate to see you like this. Just when things seemed to be getting a little better."

"Things were getting better?"

"I mean, with your mood," Yakov ventured cautiously. He seemed to realize that he had said too much.

"What was wrong with my mood?"

"I don't know, it's nothing."

"What was wrong with my mood that it was such a *mechayeh* that it was getting better?"

"Sara, let's not change the subject. You'll see someone tomorrow about the rash?"

"What was it about my mood that you didn't tell me—for how long, Yakov? But now, it's suddenly so important?"

"I'm just saying you seemed a little down. Everyone gets that way sometimes, it's nothing to be ashamed of."

"Who said anything about shame? I'm not ashamed of anything. I just wish that I didn't have this awful rash," Sara said. The tears, which she had summoned in deceit, now came in earnest. She found herself crying.

"There, there. The doctor will help you. We'll get through

mechayeh – wonderful thing (lit. "makes life")

this," Yakov said. But he seemed hesitant to embrace her. Finally he tried to put his arm around her shoulders, but Sara drew back. She left him, taking refuge in the bathroom, surrounded by white tile and porcelain.

The visit to the dermatologist went exactly as planned. Who can ever pinpoint the cause of a rash? The doctor wondered if it might be a reaction to some clothing, some new detergent maybe, but when Sara denied all these possibilities and mentioned the curious correlation with the beard, of course that had to be explored. It was odd, but not unheard of. Maybe there was a soap or shampoo Yakov used for the beard? No? Well, it could be the beard itself. Still, it seems more like something from a cosmetic or soap. Ask Yakov if he puts anything in his beard, you know, to groom it. Maybe it's that. In the meantime, he said, "I know it's difficult, but—"

Sara's heart leapt in anticipation.

"—stay away from your husband's beard until we have it sorted out."

"But, doctor—"

"I'll speak to Yakov myself," the doctor said. "If your health is endangered, that takes precedence. I'm going to prescribe you some medication for the rash. And I want you to change the soap you're using to wash your face. No cosmetics, either, for now. Come back and see me in a week."

So Sara gained her freedom. On the street, people would stare sometimes; her friends offered solace, though they also seemed afraid of catching the rash, but in reality, it was not so hideous. Sara had stopped applying the cleanser, since it no longer seemed to be necessary, and since she could always add another dose if the effects wore off. So, a few pimples. It was nothing worse than what you see on unfortunate teenagers every day. Dov Baer, Sara thought, might get zits like this within a few years, or even less. Meanwhile, Sara felt stronger than before. She looked at Yakov across the dinner table, looked at the beard when he didn't notice, and felt she had won. You are defeated, she thought as she gazed upon it. You who mastered me are now my servant. When I allow you to come, then you will come. And when I choose to be free of you, I will be free.

After three weeks in which the rash subsided only slightly, Sara and Yakov grew more resourceful in expressing their affections. Yakov became an even more zealous practitioner of oral sex, as if delighted to finally have a new challenge, a new way to fulfill the mitzvah of pleasing his wife. They could go for hours, it seemed: Sara on Yakov, Yakov on Sara, each on each other. And always, Sara in control, reminding Yakov to hold on to his beard, because the doctor says . . . It was, for Sara, a glorious time. She was enjoying the most pleasurable physical intimacy with her husband since before the children were born. It was as if Yakov's pent-up energy and frustrated love had finally found an outlet. Their lovemaking had taken on new forms, new positions, and new configurations as Yakov worked to adapt both to his poisonous facial hair and to Sara's unsightly blemishes.

Gradually, the pimples decreased. But to Sara's dismay, as the rash receded, so too did Yakov's newfound passion. Sara's face no longer mirrored Yakov's, no longer forced him to transmute his affections, and allowed to run their course, they seemed to have withered. Sara thought of reapplying the cleanser, but it seemed dangerous to do so again. And yet, even as Sara and Yakov returned to more conventional forms of lovemaking, Yakov seemed hesitant to kiss her, as if fearful of causing a recurrence of the rash. And when Sara would try to initiate oral sex, Yakov would decline. "Not today, Sara," he would say. There was no way he knew of the lie; Sara felt confident of that. So what was it? Yakov seemed—and Sara cried the first time she even thought such a thing—not to desire her as he once did, not even to love her. The "beard" was exiled from Sara's face, and with it, both Yakov's tenderness and his ardor. Sara looked at herself in the mirror and no longer had the power of tears.

One day, a few months later, Dov Baer came home early from school. The late-afternoon study session was canceled; the teacher was sick; everyone in his class had gone home. Sara had been silently crying but wiped her face clean when she heard her son's voice announce that he was home. But Dov Baer came to the open bathroom door in time to catch her.

"Hello, darling," she said.

"Hi, Mami."

Sara noticed a smudge of dirt on the boy's face. "Dov Baer, you have something on your face," she said.

"What?"

"I'm not sure. Come here."

Dov Baer stood six inches from his mother's face. Sara realized what the "smudge" was.

"Stand still," she said. She reached over to the sink, took the razor she used on her legs, and silently shaved the mustache that had just begun to grow.

THE MIKVA OF BEN SIRA'S

TRANSMIGRATION

According to the medieval book of wisdom known as the *Alphabet of Ben Sira*, its legendary hero was conceived when the prophet Jeremiah's daughter bathed in a mikva in which her father had ejaculated earlier that day. Ben Sira, master of letters and names, was thus a child of virgin birth, the son and grandson of Israel's doomsaying prophet, and the product of an unintentional incestuous union between father and daughter.

When I step into the mikva, its spiritually purifying waters filthy with bits of hair and flesh, I often think of this tale and its possibility. No doubt, anything could be floating in these unchlorinated and unfiltered waters, even the blood, spit, or seed of a previous entrant. Indeed, as I immerse my naked body in its warmed waters every week before the Sabbath, and since the water, by law, must be untreated, I do not doubt that, like Ben Sira's sister-mother, I am engaging in unintentional, forbidden intercourse with dozens of men I do not know. The irony does not escape me: the same waters that are meant to cleanse the sin of unwanted seminal emissions may convey it as well. And so, as I immerse, covering my entire body in water, I pause to consider what might be intermingled with it, and with me.

Immersion in the mikva is central to my religious life, and I perform the ritual for one reason only: to cleanse myself of the sin of homosexuality that God has seen fit to bestow upon me, and to wash clean any transgressions of thought or deed that may have transpired in the previous week. Of my proclivity to this sin there has been no doubt in my mind since I first lived in Israel fifteen years ago, when I was eighteen, to spend a year studying at a yeshiva before college. That year was meant to be a time of spiritual growth; although I had grown up in an Orthodox home, privately, many of the so-called "lesser" mitzvos were disregarded or treated lightly by my parents. Corners were cut, compromises made. I disdained my parents' casual commitment, their inability to see their transgressions for what they were, their abundant desire to explain away their own shortcomings. Fleeing their lax home for the pious life of a yeshiva in Israel was a chance to finally live as a real Torah-observant Jew.

Yet yeshiva taught me not piety but sin. As an adolescent, all sexual desire was effectively forbidden, so the fantasies I entertained about my classmates were repressed, I imagined, with no greater effort than the ones they held about women. All desires were equally constrained, and all were equally forbidden. Of course, I was troubled by my inclinations. I consulted certain trusted sources for instruction as to wet dreams, and learned of Rabbi Nachman's *Tikkun HaKlali*, a set of psalms to recite in penance after such a dream came. Yet I did not see myself as specially burdened. And in the showers at the gym or in the bunks at my summer camp, I observed myself to be no more inquisitive as to the naked bodies of my friends than they were as to each other's, or to mine.

But at yeshiva, I began to see myself as abnormal, different, and in need of repair. I was eighteen and living in a dorm room with three other boys. We were all from around New York and set to attend college after the year was over, but often we would confide in one another that, were it not for our parents' insistence, we would stay a second year, or maybe even stay forever—make aliyah and live here permanently, learning Torah in Jerusalem or one of the settlements outside it. Yet alongside this devotion, the yeshiva was like a hormonally charged locker room. In high school, my bodily interactions with other boys had been bounded by the walls of the gym and the bells of fourth period. Now, physicality was omnipresent. The place was redolent with the smells of late adolescence. The sexual tension could be felt in the air, in the *beis medrash*, in the dorms, even in the room where we ate our meals. Moreover, I learned from my roommates, my high school assumptions of universal celibacy had been false; in fact, these other boys had all been "hooking up" with certain of the girls, and if not, then "jerking off" themselves. These terms were more foreign to me than the Aramaic of the Gemara, but I quickly came to understand them, and grew alienated from these young men who had once seemed so much like me. Only I, it seemed, had scrupulously repressed my evil inclinations. During my entire adolescence, only once, in a

beis medrash – study hall
Gemara – a section of the Talmud

moment of weakness, had I pleasured myself, in the shower, and even then it seemed to happen half by accident, and was followed by weeks of *tehillim*. But, I learned, this was not the norm even among the frum boys whose *emunah* I had admired. They had all been carrying on in ways I had never imagined.

And now, in the yeshiva, the sin of Onan was omnipresent. There was little alternative; it was impossible to "hook up" under the watchful eyes of the rabbis. And as there was hardly any privacy in the yeshiva, what I had once thought of as the most secret of sins was suddenly out in the open: in the communal showers, in bathroom stalls, in beds while roommates lay awake only a few feet away. I participated— of course, I participated. I felt that if I didn't join in, my secret, my difference, would somehow be discovered. But confronted with this omnipresent eroticism, it had become impossible for me to avoid my deviant urges. I felt them all the time, swimming in a sea of male hormones, male sexuality, male bodies. It was clear what I wanted—and how that set me apart from the others. Of course, my classmates' sexual play was undeniably homoerotic, as were their facetious remarks about Shmuley's long one or Eliezer's fat one, and their supposedly sarcastic come-ons and jokes. But that was only because of the circumstances—I knew that one day, and soon, they would all go on to be happily married to women. They had no real interest in each other's bodies, whereas I was like Adam in Gan Eden, aware of my nakedness and theirs, and fearful of that knowledge being

emunah – faith

discovered. *Mi higid lekha, ki arum atah*, God says: Who told you that you were naked?

On the eve of Yom Kippur, I went to the mikva for the first time, together with the rest of the yeshiva. It struck me as a cold, dank place, too small for all of us, and only barely conforming to the halachos we had learned: the minimum size, the requirement that its waters by untouched by mechanical agency, and so forth. That first time, I learned the irony that has defined my weekly ritual ever since: that this place meant to cleanse the body of sexual sin was, itself, sexual in nature. Surrounded by naked bodies, I had to confront my sin directly, precisely in the moment of its abnegation. That first Yom Kippur, I saw more than ever before what stains clung to me, stuck to me like barnacles on the side of a ship. And as I stepped into the tiny ritual bath, already crowded with three of my classmates, I wanted nothing more than to cleanse the desire for them from my body. Yom Kippur, too, is centered around this notion of catharsis; *kapparah*, usually translated as "atonement," more literally means "cleansing." It is what must be done to any place that has become impure: scouring, uncovering hidden stains, confronting them, and, through hard effort, expunging them. I prayed that day that the mikva would do the same for me.

Afterward, I felt refreshed in a way I could not explain. I had learned in books how important the mikva had been to the Israelites in the desert, and how, often, the first building a Jewish community would build, even before the synagogue, was the mikva. I had also known that while immersion was commanded only of women, it also had been practiced by men, regularly, across hundreds of generations. But nothing had prepared me for the *feeling* of it: a sensation, and also a deep, profound knowledge, of having died and been reborn. It was as though the mikva had annihilated my sexual longings along with the residue of my sexual sin. It was indeed a return to the womb, and from it I emerged a new man, reborn, cleansed of my transgressions. And so, at the age of eighteen, I resolved to visit the mikva every week before Shabbos.

That was all many years ago, and everything about my life has changed. I am no longer in touch with my friends from yeshiva. Most did, in fact, return to America for college, and most of them are still there. They all have wives, and most, by now, children as well. In college, and for the first few years afterward, when bachelorhood was a shared condition, we would still spend time together, have Shabbos meals together. But gradually, as my friends settled into their lives, they stopped calling me, stopped needing to call me, as their new relationships supplanted the old ones, and, I supposed, they grew suspicious of me. No one ever said anything openly, but given the passage of time, and my inability to find a wife, my perversion had become, I felt, an open secret. And so when I turned thirty, I made aliyah. Here, in Jerusalem, it is less unusual for a religious man in his thirties to be single—we all have our stories, our pasts, and our *mishegas*. Here I could be seen, like Ben Azzai, as

mishegas – craziness

married to Torah, to God, to *kedusha*. And if not, then at least all of us have one idiosyncrasy in common: we've all rejected a comfortable life for a less comfortable one. Where everyone is a bit of a misfit, my own difference seems somehow to matter less.

For a while, I contemplated marriage myself and dated several women, in the nonsexual way that many Torah Jews do: a few meetings in hotels and parks, discussions of children and ritual observance, small talk about families and backgrounds. I considered the promises that some rabbis held out, that it was possible to change, and entered therapy to do so. But it was all obviously a sham. I was repulsed by the idea of sex with women, and even if I could somehow complete the sexual act thanks to the "therapy," there would still be the deception: the false vows before God, and the daily confrontation with someone who was supposed to be my lover but who would be only a kind of nemesis. Most of all, I could not force another person to live the life into which God had forced me.

Yet I knew that the "gay lifestyle" was not for me either. I experimented now and then, venturing out into their seedy bars and their mindless, pulsating dance clubs. But no matter how I tried to convince myself otherwise, I saw the darkness of sin everywhere I went. And not only the sin itself, but also the glorification of surface, sensuality, and the kind of "freedom" that exists only in the hearts of men who do not truly understand the meaning of the word. The few times I did meet men for sex were limited to

kedusha – holiness

semi-anonymous encounters—in parks, in their apartments (never in my own), and, once, at a club. At least in these acts of transgression, it was clear that we were servicing a biological need alone; there was no glorification of it, no illusions. The sex was quick, and at once mechanical and animalistic. I would immerse in the mikva later, grateful to God for my connection to Him, thankful that I had not fallen into these shadowlands of desire and filth.

I know what some would say: that this voice of reproof is not a spark of God but rather guilt, that the words of the Torah are somehow false or incomplete, that I should have surrendered my religious life for the sake of this vapid "happiness." But I know that the voice of rebuke is the same holy spark of the soul that admonishes me to do good and pursue holiness. I cannot deny it or reduce it to something less than what it is. And I am not alone: there are many frum Jews like me, fighting the same inclinations, every day waking to the same battles with the *yetzer hara*. We do not march in the parades. But what the secular Jews say is shame, we know to be the command of God. Perhaps one day, I might even find a man with whom I can share my life in purity and chastity, a true friend who loves Torah and mitzvos as much as I.

I continue to go to the mikva with complete faithfulness. It is the simultaneous expression and abnegation of my sexuality. I still feel its waters cleanse me of whatever sins I have accumulated; its all-encompassing warmth and silence return me to a state of innocence and purity. And yet the

_____

yetzer hara – evil inclination, specifically the sexual urge mikva is also a place of confrontation, like the showers at the yeshiva those years ago. Unlike in my yeshiva days, it is the only time during the week that I see other men naked, when the secret of my desire is exposed, revealed as I am. Stripping off our clothes together, I am laid bare spiritually as well as carnally. But I am not alone: though of course the act of unclothing does not have the same meaning for others, all of us—friends, fathers, sons, brothers—are naked together, and in the bath's waters, we commingle with one another. This is the intimacy that I am allowed. And of course, in fifteen years of going to the mikva, I have never witnessed or participated in any overt expression of physical sexuality.

Except once.

It was a normal Friday afternoon: the city rapidly preparing for its weekly slowing-down, people carrying shopping bags from one place to the next, the last buses making their rounds as the streets began to slowly empty of cars. I was running late, and by the time I got to the mikva, the attendant had already left, though the mikva itself was still open.

When I entered, the place was virtually empty. Only one man was in the changing area, a round-bodied and hairless man in his fifties or sixties, and he was putting on his clothes, preparing to leave. I felt a familiar blend of satisfaction and disappointment. My meditation would be easier, undistracted by naked bodies glimpsed in my peripheral vision. And yet, did I not also want those distractions? Had I not looked forward to them all through the lonely week?

I nodded perfunctorily to the man, and began to take off my clothes. As is my custom, I turned my mind to reviewing the week: my tasks at work, my plans for Shabbos, my lapses in self-control. It had been an ordinary week, with only two nights in front of the computer screen to be washed away in the water, and nothing particularly remarkable besides. Naked, I looked over my body. I had lost some weight, I noticed; my skin was pale, but summer was coming; it would turn a healthier shade soon. I walked to the shower, where I washed off bits of hair and dirt still clinging to me, making sure that nothing interrupted the contact between myself and the living waters, and looked at the two small, square pools, each about six feet long and wide. They had been heavily used that day, and showed it. But I was used to the juxtaposition of spiritual purity and physical grime, and so I chose one and entered the water and immersed my customary seven times, spending a few moments underwater each time, feeling the renewal and the peace and the quiet, making sure that none of my body protruded. I visualized an inner *mem-yood-mem*, spelling the Hebrew word for water, *mayim*. I heard its feminine, maternal sound, each *mem* the numerical equivalent of the forty *se'ah* of water needed to make a mikva valid, each forty a symbolic representation of completeness and rebirth, like the forty years in the desert and the forty days and nights on Mount Sinai. Each *mem* the womb, with the lone *yood* of my own sex suspended in between.

As I stood up from my seventh and final immersion, I was startled to see a young man stepping into the mikva—my mikva, I thought immediately, even though the other one was empty. Why? Stunned, I couldn't help but watch him.

He was beautiful—around the age I was when I first entered the mikva those many years ago—with dark brown hair, a thin frame, and those delicate, somewhat feminine features that so many yeshiva *bochurim* have; his body was smooth save for a small nest of brown pubic hair. I only glanced downward for a moment, so as not to arouse suspicion, but I was, myself, aroused, and so I quickly stepped back into the mikva's waters to conceal myself. He walked right in. He carried himself with a kind of insouciant obliviousness to his own beauty—an unconscious, unpracticed confidence that I could not duplicate even with years of effort. It was only as my eyes watched his calves gently stepping into the mikva's waters that I realized I had been staring.

Immediately I ought to have averted my eyes, gotten up, moved past the young man, and returned to the shower room. The right thing to do was clear. But I was frozen: if I got up, he would see that I was aroused, and besides, I seemed unable to move in any case, so instead I quickly ran my eyes up from his body to his face, only to find that he was looking at me, expressionless. It was still safe to leave. His face was blank; his dark hair was matted to his head. I tried to discern whether he had any *payes*, to see how religious he was, but couldn't tell.

"Hello," he said, in English, but with an Israeli accent.

"Hello," I said back, shocked that he had spoken to me. It was rare to acknowledge the presence of another person in this place, let alone to stare back, as he did. I tried to act as though nothing was unusual, though everything was. I pushed off my feet as if to casually move aside, but

I unintentionally exposed myself above the waterline. The young man looked over, then looked away and did three immersions in the mikva, quickly, seemingly without much expression or feeling. Then he rose, lifted up his feet, and floated on his back, as if he were showing off as I had done.

"Are you looking at me?" he asked.

"Sorry," I said, growing erect under the water. He moved closer.

"Do you want to touch it?"

Without thinking, I put my hand on him. Never had anything like this happened before in the mivka, and I felt myself filled with fear as well as excitement. This was wrong. But I continued. He grew rapidly in my hand.

"What's your name?" I asked.

"It doesn't matter," he said. I caressed his chest. There was a silence in the room that I had never heard there before. It was as if we were still underwater; the air seemed to be made of wool.

"You won't tell me your name?" I asked.

"It's not important."

I continued touching him. I worried that we would be caught. Unlikely: Shabbos was almost in. No one would be coming, except maybe the attendant to lock up, and we would hear him. What was I supposed to do? Everything was new. I maneuvered him so that he was standing in front of me, my body pressed up behind his. I was touching him lovingly, not lustily; I wondered if he noticed this. I felt tears begin to form. I wondered if he preferred to be touched in this way or the other way. I knew that I could not turn back.

It felt as though I had emerged from my immersions reborn into the *olam haba* in which all laws were suspended.

He reached around his back and touched me. I sighed reflexively.

"What's your name?" I asked again. He didn't answer. I wanted to know, I wanted to know if he was like me—if, perhaps, we shared a *neshama*, as the Baal Shem Tov says, with roots in the other world. I wanted to know this, to learn the essence of his being, encoded in the name. Because maybe I could save him from the years of torment I had endured, somehow to spare him our shared pain. I wanted to know him. And I realized it was not lust that I felt, now; it was a love that is *kadosh*, holy; I wanted what other Jews have when they consummate their love every Friday night—the unity on high between the Shechinah and the Holy One, and the unity here between souls, between bodies. I wanted no separation, the holy love that others take for granted, unifying the lust of the body with the thirst of the spirit.

"Tell me your name," I whispered into his ear. He only sighed. He was getting close, I could tell, as was I. But also closer to *yichud*, to unity beyond differentiation. His hand moved faster on me, his body had begun to tense. I remembered suddenly my roommates in the yeshiva, seeing who could shoot the farthest, ripping off their clothes to compete, naked, even though there was no reason they had to take off their shirts and shoes and socks, which meant, what, that they wanted it—they wanted each other completely, just as

olam haba – world to come
neshama – soul

God wants us completely, just as we must in the mikva strip away our clothes and our thoughts and sins, just as we must cleave to God and stand naked in front of Him, face-to-face as the Zohar says, by which it means, the name that is known, the secret exposed, and thus releasing the flow of the Divine love, the sustenance that comes to us from His holy foundation, falling like rain. "Tell me your name," I said urgently.

"Mendel," he said, and we shuddered together, with the exhalation of a single *aleph*, with the sigh that precedes the sigh, my head arched back in release, and I said, "Mendel," and we released into the water, and we both leaned backward in the water, and I held him as we floated in the water.

The *Alphabet of Ben Sira* does not explain the scandal of how Jeremiah's sperm came to be floating in the mikva where his daughter would later bathe. One commentator asserts that the prophet was accosted by a group of homosexuals who caused him to ejaculate into the bath. I wonder about the circumstances of this strange consummation; why a sage who had mastered the secrets of letters was conceived in such a way; and whether through those letters, what is done might be undone, and what is broken may be brought together.

THE VERSE

On the day the verse was erased, I was in bed, half-asleep, nursing a Friday-morning hangover. It was my sister who told me the news, waking me with a telephone call.

"Did you hear what happened?" she asked.

"What?"

"Check the news. Something strange has happened to the Torah."

I imagined, in my foggy, hypnagogic mind, a particular Torah: the one in the ark of the synagogue where I was bar mitzvahed twenty years ago. That Torah was *the* Torah, I assumed, sitting under fluorescent light in a small alcove, set into a blank, beige-painted wall. Had it been stolen?

"I don't get it," I said.

"There's—it's hard to explain. I just wanted to make sure you're okay. You should really—just check the news."

I was embarrassed: caught sleeping after ten on a week-day morning, while most of the city was already making money. My sister always was the responsible one. What was the news? I turned on my phone, still in a dream. I scrolled through the videos in my feed.

"Scholars across the globe are dumbfounded at what can only be described as a miraculous event—"

"It occurred shortly before the onset of the Jewish Sabbath in Jerusalem—"

"The verse reads, 'And with a man you shall not lie as with a woman; it is an abomination,' and is widely—"

"It was, ironically, on this Sabbath that the portion containing the verse was to have been—"

And there was Rabbi Yossi Baruch, bearded and bright-eyed, seeming, as always, to be in love with himself and giddy with the thought of being on television. "As the Jewish Sabbath was beginning in Jerusalem, Leviticus 18:22 inexplicably—some would say miraculously—disappeared from every extant Torah scroll on the planet," he said, as if any of what he was saying made sense. "Not every text of the Torah," he continued. "Only the scrolls. The verse that has disappeared is—or perhaps I should say *was*—generally understood as the biblical injunction against homosexuality. But you must understand, every letter, every stroke of every letter in the Torah, is extremely important. Every word contains a wealth of hidden meanings, legal implications, even mystical significance. Each is a spark of wisdom that leads to a plenitude of understandings—"

I knew Rabbi Baruch, even met him once. He'd made a fortune explaining Jewish traditions on sexuality. He'd always tried to talk around the gay issue, knowing it was bad for his public profile to toe the Orthodox line, but since he was ideologically committed to that same line, he couldn't exactly *not* toe it either.

I looked up from the phone and out my window. A cloud was passing by. Twenty blocks south, Rabbi Berel Weintraub perceived it to be an evil omen.

That cloud is too low. It is a sign of judgment. The birth pangs of the Messiah. Everything must be interpreted. He stroked his white beard and slumped back into his desk chair, which rolled to the wall. He had been on the phone continuously since ten—5:00 p.m. in Jerusalem, just as the Sabbath was beginning, when the miracle happened and the phones began to ring. Now it was almost noon, and still the phones rang. Chava was his only source of strength, Chava who now parried on the telephone with rabbis and community leaders from across the country, all demanding an answer from the esteemed scholar—an answer that Rav Weintraub knew he could not give.

Rav Weintraub's first thought had been: For this? Two thousand years of waiting, and God gives us a sign *for this?* Because he knew it was a sign, and that it was from God. It was not, as the *sonei yisroel* said, some ridiculous plot involving global elites. This was an act of the supernatural. As if anyone, let alone the perverts, could sneak into all the museums, the genizahs, the locked *aronei kodesh* in a thousand shuls across the world? And then perfectly erase, without a single trace, and without even a gap, a verse written in permanent ink on parchment? The verse didn't just disappear, leaving a blank space—*it seemed to have never existed at all.* Berel had seen it with his own eyes, as soon as the first story broke, now almost two hours ago. He ran to the shul, the *gabbai* opened up the *Sefer Torah*, and there, where the

aronei kodesh – arks
gabbai – synagogue assistant

words *ve'et zachar lo tishkav mishkevei isha, to'evah hi* used to be, now there was nothing. The Torah went straight from *ani Adonai* in verse 21 to *uve-chol behema* in verse 23. The section break a few lines down was larger than it had been, but that was all. No, this was not a conspiracy, it was a miracle—but what kind of miracle? Berel wondered, thinking now of his young son and how he wanted so to protect him from the world. He knew that when a man of faith is presented with overwhelming evidence that contradicts his faith, he nonetheless chooses belief. This is the meaning of faith, that it is the ground of reality that stays true despite that which shifts. Explanation may fail; even expression may fail. But ultimately the man of faith knows in his deepest heart that he believes. And there is love there, and rest.

In their beautiful restored apartment in a southern neighborhood of Jerusalem, Yehudit Shalev opened a bottle of champagne and called out to her wife Nomi.

"What are you doing?" Nomi asked in Hebrew, entering the room when she heard the pop of the cork.

"I'm celebrating. Kiss me with the kiss of your lips—your love is sweeter than wine." And they kissed.

"You and your religious songs, Yudit."

"Nomi, this is what we have wished for all our lives."

"Maybe you wished, with your love of the old superstitions," Nomi replied, breaking the embrace. "But I have no use for their Torah, their verse, or their God. And now, uninvited, he has broken into my house and insisted that I recognize him. Which I do not!"

"You're being crazy," Yehudit replied. "Their God has

spoken on our side! The entire world has changed!"

"Great, and now we will hear about nothing except the miracle! The miracle this, the miracle that! The Messiah is coming! What, so now every other verse in the Torah is true because this one was made false? The world was created in six days? And what about *us*, Yudit? Women, I mean. Now we have no rights, no names, no humanity? Now our blood is impure again? Now we must obey our husbands? Why didn't their god speak about *us*?"

"God *did* speak about our humanity," pleaded Yehudit. "Because the Torah must change, has to change. This is just one example! God has taken out this verse to tell us to reinterpret all the others, the cruel ones, the evil ones. Nomi, somewhere there's a man, right now, someone who used to believe that we were *evil*—and he's in *doubt*, Nomi! Do you see the irony? He's in *doubt* because *God has spoken*."

I next saw my cousin Eliezer, who was one such Jew. Throughout Shabbos services at his shul in the old ultra-Orthodox part of Jerusalem, there had been a hush over the *kahal*. A man had come in shouting, right as *Kabbalat Shabbat* was set to begin: a *shammos* had rolled the Torah to the next *parsha* and noticed something odd, and then— check for yourselves! Then another man, with the same outrageous tale. So the Torah had been unwrapped—the rov himself had authorized it—and, sure enough, the verse was gone. Like it never existed! If this was an act of human beings, it was the greatest blasphemy ever to be perpetrated. The death penalty would not be enough. And to make

shammos – synagogue "beadle"

such a disgusting point, such a vile point! The kahal had its suspicions about who in their community might indulge in such . . . abominations. And if they were responsible . . .

But, like Berel, Eliezer had to admit that this could be no act of human beings. This was not difficult for him; though he was not ultra-Orthodox like most of the men in his shul, he loved Israel, and the people Israel, and understood that God intervened in human affairs all the time. God steered the bullets in the Yom Kippur War, guided the missiles against the Arabs who sought to destroy us. And if Jews suffer, it is because God wills it, and because through our sins we ourselves had earned it. And when the *Bnei Yisroel* are protected, then clear and convincing evidence can be marshaled for the direct intervention of G-d, if only one is patient and careful enough to interpret.

But still *this* verse! The Rambam had taught that in the time of the Messiah, some mitzvos would endure and others would be set aside. So this one mitzvo was so important to merit Divine intervention? It was God who wrote the Torah, God who taught the interpretations of the Torah. So what now? Of course, no one knew anyone who actually engaged in this sin. There were misfits in the community, like Anschel, who never married and had lived with his parents until they died. People spoke about him. But that was all *loshon hora*; no one had any proof. Now Eliezer looked around his apartment. The candles had been lit for Shabbos, and his wife Chana had prepared the table as she did every week. But the davening at shul had been perfunctory, almost silent, and

Bnei Yisroel – Jews

even now, when the Karliners' kids should be screaming on the other side of the paper-thin wall, everything was quiet. It was as if everyone in Jerusalem had been stunned. What was next? Eliezer wondered.

A few blocks away in Jerusalem I saw Rina Levy, just over thirty, who had finally chosen to marry last year, after ten years of meeting stupid men, pushy men, men who didn't seem to shower in the morning. She knew her betrothed was gay; it was obvious. But she had watched her friends accept increasingly defective husbands, each with flaws of their own. This one never looked you in the eye, that one had no *seichel*, and these defective men married good, smart girls. So was being gay so much worse? Menachem was kind. Rina knew he fantasized when he was with her, she knew not to say anything about it, she knew he felt guilty—she knew all of this, and she accepted him because both their families were frum and she loved the lives they all led; she was unwilling to give this up. So when this attractive, kind, gentle man approached her, a little old to be single, a little quirky, like a lot of the *olim* in Jerusalem, she accepted him. Here was a man who could hold an intelligent conversation, who had a job and a sense of humor. He kept the mitzvos, even went to the mikva before Shabbos each week. Everyone has an inner demon they wrestle with; this wrestling is what makes religion possible. So when Rina heard the news—her mother had called her in a sort of apocalyptic panic—she instantly thought of her husband, and cried. Whether the

seichel − intelligence
olim − immigrants to Israel

tears were for his liberation, or hers, or for the loss of the arrangement that had met their needs so gently, Rina could not be sure.

In the beit midrash of the Jewish Theological Seminary, only a few miles from my apartment, Torah scrolls were being closely inspected by Professor Michael Wigand's rabbinical students. "Check every letter of every verse," he instructed them again. "Don't trust yourself that you know every letter." This is how I can be of use, Wigand thought, as his students pored over the scrolls. Leave the speculation to the speculators. What I can do is make sure we've got the text right. What if there's more missing that we don't know about? It could be more subtle—a letter here or there, or a word. Let the others guess as to what it means. I can tell you what it says.

Rachel looked around at the other students in the beit midrash, all apparently in shock but still somehow diligently checking over every line of the Torah, as if Michael Wigand's scholarly rigor had any bearing on what had just occurred. All of them had spent their young careers in dialogue with sacred text, navigating the tension between the words on the page and our evolving conceptions of human nature, science, ethics. While the words are on the page, Rachel thought, it's up to us to make the Torah a living document. *Lo ba-shamayim hi*, she had been taught: the Torah isn't in heaven, and we don't listen to voices. We listen to reason and to conscience. Now the rules were suddenly thrown out the window, but her friends were still playing the old game, cross-checking every line of the Torah. They can't handle it, Rachel thought. This is how they sublimate their terror.

"Is this the God in which we believe?!" Rabbi Dr. Harold Millman asked no one in particular as he strode into the beit midrash, startling Rachel and several other students. "We have already changed our interpretation of this law—I published an article twenty years ago arguing exactly that! But to accept that God has acted—and that God has chosen to act after Auschwitz and Stalin, after Hiroshima and the Middle Passage? This is unconscionable! The God in which I believe resides in the human heart, from whence we hear the voice of conscience. That is the voice telling me to temper judgment with *hesed*, with lovingkindness. But this? This lowers us all. It dehumanizes us, reduces us to children who have no choice—*no choice*—but to obey the father's will. Is this what the Israelites felt when, encamped under Sinai, it seemed that God was speaking directly and only to them? Are we infants now, as then?"

Overlaid with these rabbis was the image of a likeness of a Catholic priest, clad in black, alone in his study, his face in his hands. Unlike many of his brethren, he had mastered his lusts that were *para physin* for forty years, not once engaging in *peccatum mortale*, despite many opportunities to do so, mastering his desires to the point that they were no longer even desires, as the Church taught, his will stronger than the body, crushing it. And now, for what? The priest thought back to his own youth, when as an altar boy, he felt Father Monahan embrace him, and he knew that he would have given his body over to the priest had he asked. And yet, he hadn't asked, making the embrace pure, holy. To master one's urges, to yoke them to a holy cause, was the greatest service. To love only God, because all other love was forbidden. How could this be taken away?

This image was engulfed in flames.

And in the fire I saw what had happened. I saw Sholom Berger, a young Hasidic man pleading for a miracle at the dawn *hashkama minyan*—silently, so that no one else would hear, but desperately seeking to will his petition into action: "Please, God, make the verse disappear. Just make it gone. I wish it would disappear. I wish it never existed. I wish I could be what you want me to be, but I can't. I wish I could be normal, but you won't let me be. You won't let me, as much as I have tried. You have created me as you have. You force me to disobey you. You made me, and you push me away. *Asher yatzar ha'adam b'chokhmah*, you have made me in your wisdom. Why? *Ribbono shel Oilam*, I'll tell everyone, I'll tell my mother, I'll come clean, but don't force me to rebel against you any longer. I don't want to leave you. I want to love you. Just make the verse—one verse, one line, eight words, twenty-eight letters—disappear, and it would all be as it should. Twenty-eight letters! Make them disappear, God, unwrite the verse. Say you didn't mean it. It was an aberration. A misunderstanding. The scribes got it wrong, they didn't hear clearly. *Avinu she-Bashamayim*, make it disappear, let me love you as you have commanded, *b'chol l'vavcha, uv'chol nafshesha, uv'chol me'odecha*, God, with all my heart, with all my soul, with all my might. If you won't change me,

Ribbono shel Oilam – Master of the Universe
Avinu she-Bashamayim – Father in Heaven

change the verse. If only it didn't exist!"

And then I saw a curious thing. I saw the letters of Sholom's prayer fly upward and unite with a chant, an incantation, from halfway around the world. It came from a circle—no, a writhing, twisting mass of people, dancing around a giant pole they had placed into the earth: the *Asherah*, the Maypole, rooted in the earth. Some in the mob were dancing, some were drumming, some were writhing in embrace with one another, some were naked, some were arrayed in robes and leather and jewels; there was delight and song, chanting, circling the pole, rolling in the mud and the dirt of the earth—and suddenly there was a silence that descended, a hush as a magic unfurled itself, a great exhaling of spirit-moss from the earth-mouths, a giant sigh of primordial sound: a spell, born of seed and breath, and this great *ahhhh* ascended through the pole and into the sky and mingled with the letters of Sholom's prayer, and at that instant, a *kol demamah dakah*, a quivering, faint voice was heard in Sholom's soul, as if answering his prayer: *ahhhh*, and Sholom sighed, *meyn*.

Amen, the *bat kol* had answered. Your fight is concluded, and all is well.

And with that, Sholom stood still, quieting his *shuckling*, his body coming to rest, his heart knowing its own *shlemut*, its own completion and sufficiency. Nothing more needed to be done. No one at the shul had heard Sholom's prayer, and no one knew that it had been answered, and not even Sholom

bat kol -- Divine voice
shuckling -- swaying in prayer

knew what marriage of sense and sex had accomplished this thing, had combined to change the Torah.

It is told that the gates of heaven open to a broken heart, as when God heard the cries of Ishmael in the wilderness. But the secret, which Sholom was not yet worthy of hearing, is that delight too may force them open; that the gates are not in heaven but on earth; that the portals of a thousand *heikhalot* reside in the vines of sacred plants and the bark of sacred trees, the acacia wood in the desert and the ark, the tree of life, the Asherah, happiness, ecstasy, joy.

These images dissolved, returning to their supernal source in the womb of Divine wisdom. I looked over next to me, and there was my lover, Asher, his head on the pillow, lightly snoring. As I looked at him, he woke up and smiled.

"I love you," he said.

"I love you too," I answered.

God, otherwise, was silent.

heikhalot – heavenly palaces

THE NIGHT WATCHMAN AND THE
HUNDRED THOUSAND GOLEMS

In the silence between three and five in the morning, by the light of the electric chandeliers of 250 Central Park West, I, Nicholas Zomanski, read zealously from the esoteric traditions of the world. Avidly I pore over the theosophical meditations of Madame Blavatsky, the yogic sciences of chakras and incarnations and propensities, ancient myths of Indigenous peoples that tell of entities in constant communication with humans and animals alike. But of all these, I cherish most the permutations, symbols, and tales of the Kabbalah. Many nights, after the last drunk, rebellious children of the building's psychiatrists and brokers have at last staggered home to their well-appointed apartments, when the night grows entirely silent except for the wind of a few passing taxicabs, I have pored over the secret deeds of sages, sorcerers, seers, and prophets. I have immersed in the Zohar's abstruse speculations into the mystery of the Divine form, seen poetic visualizations of the supernal palaces, practiced the yogic exercises of the ecstatics. But even among these, my favorites are the stories of the mystics themselves: of Talmudic masters causing trees to ignite as they expound mystical secrets; of medieval rabbis creating men from dust, only to have them run amok; of prophets gone mad and speaking in tongues. Even when my work is complete, even when I walk home on the newly crowded Manhattan streets, even when I am engaged in the mundane activities of sustaining my solitary existence, I am accompanied by the tales and ideas that form the architecture of my solitude. Others have appointments and relationships and objects they acquire, but the palaces of the mind are more opulent and more expansive.

I know how I appear to you: a night watchman (the antiquated term still used within the wood-framed walls of 250 CPW), a single man in his mid-fifties, largely alone. To you I know I may seem like one who has been defeated by life. I have worked as a doorman, security guard, valet, and even, in my younger and stronger days, as a bellhop at one of the city's well-regarded hotels, where I would lug, drag, lift, and port the luggage of the elite. But this work suits me, for it sets me free from extraneous obligations and interchange. Even as a child, much of the social world was inexplicable to me: the social codes of young adulthood, with its fractal hierarchies that multiplied in infinite complexity; or the ways in which one was supposed to disclose but not disclose, to share precisely the information about oneself that was least revealing while concealing anything that would actually constitute communication; or what it meant to dress, groom, and speak in ways that, in some subtextual and symbolic way, would correctly convey one's own status, worth, wealth, and value. Even in all their baroque layers, levels, and correspondences, I find the esoteric secrets of Kabbalah, freemasonry, illuminism—even Mormonism and Scientology—far easier to discern than the the occult rules of society with which most people, apparently, are somehow automatically conversant. Fortunately, in my work, the ways in which one is to dress and speak are clear and prescribed, governed by rules I have mastered over decades of experience. Those rules enable me to interact with the ordinary world. But as for my inner reality, I live in a world adjacent to that of most people, one interpenetrated with unseen forces that others cannot perceive simply because they are too busy chattering with one another about nonsense.

It was always this way for me. I grew up two hours' drive north of the city. My parents were organic farmers who sold their honey, syrup, jams, and breads to tourists visiting Ulster County on weekends. They composted; they wore hemp; they danced barefoot at gatherings at a nearby retreat center. I was raised with only natural materials: no plastic toys, no screens. And so I learned to read early, and loved fairy tales, especially the unvarnished ones, with their murder and cannibalism and gore. Naturally, my parents found this disturbing and tried to steer me toward wholesome stories with multicultural characters and positive ethical values, the more they did so, the deeper I delved into fantasy, science fiction, mythology, horror, and entire genres of which my well-meaning parents were quite unaware. As I grew older, this evolved quite naturally into esotericism, magic, and mysticism, with their intricate expositions of correspondences, elementals, and, of course, the permutations of letters and numbers. The Zomanskis, may their memories be for a blessing, were secular Jews, and tried to steer me toward more practical spiritualities: Zen meditation, veganism, existential philosophy, crystal healing. I read Kahlil Gibran at puberty, Sartre and D. T. Suzuki at sixteen. But even these sages seemed to speak only of the surface ripples on the pond of reality; I was attracted to the depths. Precisely those qualities that made me less fluent with the languages and ways of human sociality gave me capacities to explore the hidden structures of reality, the ways in which the visible and invisible intertwine. And as the years have passed, I have remained essentially the same, despite the rounding of this body and receding of my hair. Many people, most people it seems, experience phases of life, with friendships, romances, marriages, children, families, careers, relocations. I do not. To me, these are the mere surfaces of things: appearances, mirages, utterly pointless details about how a person looks or feels. The meanings of life lie elsewhere.

I love the quietest hours of the night, a deathly, cottony silence in the air, with only the slightest murmuring hum of the city's perpetual drone in the background. Then, in the peaceful stillness, I am able to pore over the mystical extrapolations of Abulafia, the disciples of the Holy Lion, and the scandalous proofs of the new Messiah propounded by the prophet Nathan of Gaza; and oh, the tales of the miracle-working Baal Shem Tov, the cave-dwelling Shimon Bar Yochai, and the mage Honi the Circle Maker, who was said to have brought rain by drawing a circle and standing inside it. But of all these, my greatest hero is the Maharal of Prague, the famous Rabbi Loew. A genius, a scholar, and also the master of the most notorious golem in all the Kabbalah, the one that, people said, still lies dormant in the attic of the old Prague shul, waiting to be reanimated by a spell. The Maharal's mystical speculations were legendarily complex, and his reputation as a master of the magical Kabbalah was unimpeachable. Like me, he was not entirely of this world; there always seemed to be something the stories weren't telling.

So you can perhaps understand my joy when, one late autumn Sunday, I obtained a rare collection of tales of the Maharal, printed onto what were now yellow, thin pages between navy leather bindings. (Years ago, I undertook the tedious work of learning Hebrew, and while I am still no master of the sacred tongue, I can slowly, with the aid of a dictionary, read such texts in their original language.) A find! I could hardly wait for the next night shift to begin. I allowed myself small peeks—a *Rabbi Loew had delved too deep* here, a *warm glow of the Shabbos candles* there. But I waited to really begin until the familiar silences took over the building's deserted lobby. And then I read. In one tale, Rabbi Loew used his golem to defend the shul from rampaging enemies, terrifying them with the strength of the artificial man. In another, he trounced a local bishop at a disputation, proving beyond a doubt that Jesus could not have been virgin-born and that the Messiah had not yet arrived. Please understand: to make a golem is proof that one has mastered the workings of creation, the *ma'aseh bereisheit*, in the holy tongue. The better Kabbalists eschewed performing these sorts of tricks

golem – artificial human made by a Kabbalist

in public, but it is said that in private, they all had golems of their own. But Rabbi Loew's mastery of the secret arts had a different purpose: to defeat the brutishness of the enemy.

In one story, a comic tale called "The Golem's Golems," the Maharal's golem attempts to create a golem for itself: a golem's golem. The golem innocently repeats the Maharal's magical incantations, but instead of animating a lump of clay, the golem mistakenly enchants one of the Maharal's chairs, which begins to speak in a human voice and comically complain that it has been woken up from a deep slumber, and could someone please tell the Rabbi to get *up* once in a while, walk around, go outside. *And, while you're at it,* the chair continues, *could you please push me away from this table, whom I have for so long despised?* So, the golem next animates the table, who argues bitterly against that obstreperous and stuck-up little chair—who did he think he was, after all? A fight ensues, and so the golem quickly animates the *shtender,* which has been holding one of Rabbi Loew's heaviest books of sacred lore, to mediate the dispute. But the shtender has his own complaints: *Why did you animate me? What do I know? I'm just a shtender! I don't want to know from your troubles! I ache from all of Rabbi Loew's heavy books!* The golem is soon overwhelmed, like the Sorcerer's Apprentice in the popular tale, but without the human judgment even to know that things are going wrong: he, after all, is an automaton too, more like the artificial intelligences of our own day than the magicians of an earlier one. Finally, the Maharal himself appears just in time to save his home (and his furniture)

shtender – book stand

from ruin, and to deactivate all of the golems the golem had inadvertently created.

I finished this story in a creaking old chair of my own, placing my hands on my wooden desk to rise up from it. It was 3:15 in the morning, as quiet as usual, yet everything in the lobby seemed to gleam: the oak paneling, the *nouveau riche* equestrian paintings on the wall, the floor tiling in need of renovation. I paced back and forth under the fluorescent bulbs of the light fixtures. Imagine! That through the proper manipulations of letters, consciousness could be created, that humans could imitate God even in the act of creating life itself! It was an interpenetration of worlds: the word made flesh. In a way, it was a kind of revenge! The immaterial imposed onto the physical, a re-enchantment of the earth.

Looking around the lobby newly aglow, I had a realization: I believe it. I felt it in my heart, a place unscoured by reason, and immune from doubt; I felt it intuitively, deep inside my soul: materialistic science is wrong, and this is real. The myth of the golem, the man-made man, could not simply be a pile of lies. And the truth to which it obliquely gestured, the kernel inside of the shell, was this: everything is potentially conscious, potentially alive. All around us, everywhere, were sparks of the great shattering of God, and all of these sparks were yearning to be animated, to be interpreted, to speak.

After all, if one could *unintentionally* create a golem, not in the farcical mode of the Maharal's golem, but in a way that the author of the story dares not say aloud—if one could do this, then the preparation of the clay, the molding of it, even the selection of clay itself as opposed to a table or a chair—none of this mattered. There must be golems all around us, latent, waiting to be born out of furniture, papers, even food. After all, what had the Maharal's golem done but simply activate the consciousness of the objects around him already? He didn't make the shtender; the shtender was conscious even before the golem's efforts. So everything created, by man or God, must likewise have a soul latent within it. All of it was *alive*. And if the Maharal's chair could become enchanted, if it too had a soul, waiting to be expressed, why not my reading table as well? Everything, everywhere, had a soul of its own hiding within—silent, but not dead.

Suddenly, the doorbell buzzed, its harsh insectoid blare splintering the silence. It was Dakota Macintyre, from 6F, teenage daughter of Amanda and Charles, senior at Trinity—now barely able to steady herself against the glass pane of the door. I buzzed her in.

"Omigod," Dakota said, "thank you so much." She staggered toward the elevator.

"Here, let me help you," I said, and soon enough, I was bracing her with my arm, as if she would fall right over without me.

Dakota tried to focus her hazy blue eyes. She stopped walking for a moment, and there was an awkward pause as she leaned over toward me. "You're—"

"And you're drunk," I interrupted, turning back her advance and walking her to the elevator bank. She stank of—what was it?—gin. Juniper. Coriander. The constitutive elements made themselves known. Everything is worthy of notice, for everything may be interpreted.

"Good night, Ms. Macintyre," I said as I half pushed her into the elevator.

"And good night to you, Mister, uh, hahaha." The girl laughed as the doors closed in front of her.

It was as if a storm had suddenly broken in a quiet night, but then, just as soon, it passed. There was life, and then there was not, and yet, what is the human soul but a phenomenon of the brain? And what is the brain but an arrangement of proteins and cells? We are matter too, Dakota Macintyre neither more nor less than this door, this garbage pail. There are golems all around us, within us, all the time— every device that we create, every bit of furniture we carve from trees, every voice we hear inside of our minds—all of these objects are latent golems, the hallucination no less real than the reality. What was "Dakota Macintyre" but the sequences of the Divine light organized in such and such a way, no different from my own in essence, only varying in configuration. And this was the secret: the sparks can speak. With the right magical formulae or Divine names, they might become enchanted—but this enchantment is really nothing more than the awakening of what is already present in the thing itself! This raised desk, I thought, has a consciousness. It too is a golem. This red carpet, these dusted and gleaming doors. What are they saying?

"Hello?" I said aloud. But I heard nothing.

I spent the remainder of the evening concentrating in meditation; I focused on joining the letters of the Divine name one to another; I quieted my mind, trying to attune my soul to the voices around me. And yet still I heard nothing. The night passed.

The next day, I slept less than usual and awoke in the midafternoon to resume my meditation at home. I concentrated only on the minutest sensations, kept still for hours at a time, cotton stuffed in my ears. When I arrived at work, I kept my speech to a minimum and resumed my meditation whenever possible. Following the regimen of Abulafia, I ate very little, impoverishing my soul, abstaining from carnal pleasures. And I did this for six days and six nights before I heard.

It was 3:00 a.m., nearly a week to the minute from my first revelation. I was sitting perfectly still, the chair not creaking, the air hardly moving, my mind alert and attuned. Suddenly, out of nowhere, without warning or provocation, I heard language—unmistakably!

We're all here to help, they said. *Just put us to use.*

Were I not exhausted by the fasting, I would have jumped out of my chair. (Ah! Now we understand the rationale for these renunciations!) This was not talking to myself, or hearing my own thoughts as if aloud—this was something different. And of course, what they said made sense! Of course, once created, golems want to serve! It is, after all, their *raison d'être*, their reason for being—golems want to help. Telephones, toothbrushes, back supports, they all want to be *used*. Of course! Just put us to *use*. Every human being has a purpose for living—even if we don't know what that purpose is, we are part of the chain of being, each a concatenation of uncountable causes and conditions, and each of those a fractal elaboration and expression of the permuted letters of creation, and this is what we are, we and everything else. And if there is a singular unifying aspect of all that has evolved to be, it is precisely that: to *be*, and to cause more beings to be, whether in reproduction or creation or speculation or, well, the crafting of a golem! Why suppose these artificial lives were any different? They too want to *be*! To sing the fourfold song of all that is, to *function*. The pen cries out to spill its ink in letters or art. The wastepaper basket cheerfully straightens up to accept bank receipts and banana peels. *Use us!* they all say. We're here to help!

Now I opened my eyes and looked around the lobby, elated, in a kind of rapturous joy. All of these objects! And all formed by the great *yotzer or*, the former and shaper of light, through human agency, multiplied and manifold, and with this: with the intention to support life, to enable more *being*, more light—it was a joy! Calendars, soap, sidewalks, electrical sockets—all holy and alive and conscious of their oneness on the plane of *atzilut* precisely by manifesting the great diversity of *asiyah*! The elevators danced in a ballet, up and down! The newspaper—pulp and ink, arrayed into useful meaning! What a miracle! I remained in this state of ecstasy, like a torch lit by the light of the intellect, until the rays of the light signaled the coming end of my shift in the lobby. On my way home, the streets and sidewalks of Manhattan were newly radiant, like the brightness of the

atzilut – emanation
asiyah – the physical world

firmament, with dancing *seraphim* and *ophanim* garbed in the clothing of parking signs and dry cleaners. I slept for just a few hours, waking the next evening as the sun was setting, greeting my trusty alarm clock like an old friend. I was surrounded by love! The clock welcomes me into the world of magic, the bedspread keeps me warm, the hairbrush tidies my hair and readies me for work—what communion! The frying pan gleefully heated an egg, the spoon happy to be of service. All the things around me were awake, and I felt their joy at being of use. I decided to take on a new, secret name: *Yishmael*, for I hear the voices of all God's manifestations. and I thought, may I be like Rabbi Yishmael, who like me ascended from the world to the Divine palaces! And I thought: this name will be shared between me and the secret living things whom I hear. At home, at work, on the street, all around me was the vibrating presence of a hundred thousand golems, not yet granted the power of human speech, but alive and speaking nonetheless, in a way that none of these supposed sophisticates with their briefcases and tote bags could even comprehend. Indeed, the briefcases were more fulfilled, more connected to the truth of their existence and the layered realities of their happenstance, than the men who swung them from tired arms. Now I began to hear the golems even without concentrating—one time, walking home, I was stopped on the street by a shout from a newspaper box: *Hello, brother! See these papers I've got inside? Want one?*

But I began to hear other voices. I heard plastic cups

seraphim and *ophanim* – types of angels

silently cry when they were thrown away after only one use. *Six months I've waited since being formed in the factory overseas, and now two seconds pass, and it is over; I have an eternity to linger on!* I heard luggage complain when Mrs. Weinberg on the second floor blamed her suitcase for not rolling properly. *It was your fault the way you pulled me; why do you punch me when I was only trying to help?* All around me were golems wishing to serve, yet horribly mistreated by their ignorant human owners, who discarded them at the first sign of the slightest flaw, who failed to recognize the intelligences in their midst. It was a travesty—no, a tragedy! It was an outrage! Appliances, papers, envelopes crying out in agony! For every magazine fortunate enough to be read, there were dozens recycled without ever being opened! For every bit of food that brought joy to a hungry boy or girl, there were pounds of waste thrown into heaps, fruit rotting at bodegas, spoiled fish in the dumpster that never had the chance to make it to the table. I began to feel my heart breaking. All around me, there was more suffering than joy. Even ecstasies are only temporary interruptions in this endless drone of pain.

I realized what I must do: like the tzaddik, the bodhisattva, the Christ, the shaman, I must care for these motes of consciousness, I must console them. The best way would be to speak back to them in the ancient holy language in which they were created; to know them, communicate with them, commune with them. But while I could read the letters and words of sacred text, still I was no Rabbi Loew or Rabbi Yishmael. I had not learned to combine letters into magical formulae that would animate the inanimate and enable them to be saved. So I tried speaking directly.

"What is it you want?" I asked a plastic bottle crying in the garbage. "I'm sorry that they threw you away, but I have no more room in my apartment for you. The dump won't be so bad. Maybe a homeless man will adopt you! Where is it that you would like to sleep tonight?" But my offering went unanswered, perhaps even unheard; without access to the sacred letters, I could not be sure. I spoke, pleaded, entreated. I saved as many golems as I could, nurturing them at home and in closets at the building, but they said only what they said; they did not converse with me; they did not answer. What must I do?

Meanwhile, my job—Nicholas's job, not mine, not Yishmael's, I had no need for that now—had become unendurable. Walking back and forth was torture. Whenever I would pass by a dumpster, it was like a scene of carnage; I could hear the howls and moans of half-decayed golems, the wasting away of matter inanimate. It was awful! And at work, they said I was talking to the lightbulbs—but of course I was! They were screaming! Human speech became even more incomprehensible to me than before. Anyway, I preferred the company of my notebook, who wished she could have hosted better prose than my rambling notes, but at least respected me (and who, it should be noted, had a special fondness for the green pen, which she had adored for years and which I was only too happy to bring to her, pressing its body into her own, engraving letters of black fire on white fire, like the very words of holy writ). Of course I preferred this notebook to the banalities of O'Neill, the superintendent, or Sarzotti, the endocrinologist. Once, Sipes in 2E called downstairs to complain that someone seemed to be having an argument at two in the morning, and could I please tell them to cut out all the racket? "Just wait," I whispered to the umbrella stand. "We'll settle this tomorrow."

Finally, the building set me free of my old Nicholas-skin, which I barely noticed amid the din of a delivery of happy, fresh groceries; except that I knew the painful truth, which they as yet did not, that many (even most) of them would never be eaten. They would, if they were lucky, be composted, but more likely than not would simply be thrown away. I wanted to warn them, and almost did, but thought better of it; better for them not to know, to maintain their innocent, childlike hope. Anyway, there were now plenty of golems at home, since I had rescued some of the most dear to me, to nourish and care for them, to give them purpose and love and even the pleasure of utilization. What of the innocent dozens of eggs that never get taken out of their containers and are thrown away when their expiration dates come and go? What of paper and plastic bags, created, used once—so brief their intercourse with humanity!— and thrown away to rot for years? If I could only master the right combinations of letters to enchant the sleeping golems, give them the power of speech and movement, I could ease their pain, salve their loneliness. I would make everyone hear what I, Yishmael, could hear, so they could perceive our created objects for the sentient souls they were, and treat them less frivolously. I tried and tried to perform the meditations I had read about in books, I attempted to pronounce the unifications of letters, even the unifications of the seventy-two-letter name of God, but to no avail: perhaps my Hebrew was improperly inflected, or perhaps the spells were bad, but for whatever reason, nothing happened, save the relentless increase in the din of the disused. So I began to shout, to beg; I plunged myself into piles of milk cartons, discarded electronics, boxes of microwave dinners; I cried with them, able to hear but unable to help. But at least I can be their companions, like the Divine presence with us in exile. I can say unto them: I know of your hidden vitality, I sense your pain, I share your dread of onrushing oblivion! And I will comfort you, and keep you company, and bring you salvation! I was engaged in this holy labor day and night, until the police came upon me and, failing to understand, pulled me away from the sacred service and took me to a place where they said I would be safe. But it didn't matter; I would talk to the straps and the gurney, I could listen to the pillows and the sheets, for everywhere there are places to rest, and a thousand sleeping golems to fill any void.

THE ASCENT OF

CHANA RIVKA KORNFELD

I am here and not here.
I feel the cold tile of the floor, the same tile we all have in this part of Jerusalem. My husband Eliezer is looking over me. I can also hear his thoughts. He is seeing the brown shingles of a house in Plainview, Long Island, where he had lived as a child, thirty years ago. He is remembering how he had reacted when the other kids didn't play according to the rules; he is seeing himself smash the buildings they had built against his wishes.
What a strange thing has taken place. I have a television on top of me.
Eliezer is looking down at me, a thin coat of sweat under his arms, around his shoulders, and on the crown of his head, beneath his thinning hair and under the knitted kippah fastened to it. He had been watching, as always, the news. He believes that the conflicts engulfing the Jewish people are the birth pangs of the Messiah, the advent of a time of war and confusion before the Temple will be rebuilt and the enemies of Israel cast out. Soon, he told me once, maybe this summer.
Our lives have changed. Mine is about to end. Eliezer was wrong: the true redemption wouldn't have to do with

horsemen and apocalypse. It would be so secret that few would even know it had occurred. It would be so subtle that only the attentive could perceive it. For most, the malls would remain open; everything would be as it was. For those few who perceived, all would be new. This was the promise of the forgotten Messiah of the past, and his faithful believers. "The leftists," Eliezer had shouted, "the antisemites, the perverts." Eliezer was in a rage, as he had been many times before. I came into the room and I saw that he had gotten up off the sofa and was standing in front of the flat screen of the television, picking it up as if to smash it like Moshe with the tablets, except this lasted only a moment, because he didn't see me in his rage and I couldn't move away in time and the sharp edge of the television hit me instead and knocked me to the floor and I tasted blood and the screen did drop and shattered and the shards scattered and with them the light. I am here and not here.

Perhaps there is a One who is responsible for all that happens. Eliezer's anger, the politicians, the television news. The moment was a confluence of events, a chance encounter of a thousand causes. Some would call it an "accident." I heard Eliezer use the word in his mind. It was an accident. As if to deny that there is a judge and justice. Blessed be the true judge, I say for myself. And was it an accident, that I stayed with him through these years of childlessness and endless, spiraling anger? All his fitful rustling in bed, his complaints about his pointless job at the call center, his shouting at me or the neighbors or the news. I stayed because there was no better option. Even now I can feel the anger rising within him, as if this was something that had happened to him instead of to me, or that it was the leftists' fault, the antisemites, the perverts.

I see Eliezer as a little child, five years old, teased and beaten up by the older boys. I see him as a teenager at the moment he learned his friend—really just an acquaintance—had been killed by a terrorist. All these moments congeal in him: the pure, hot fire of rage. I join the list of his victims: doors, appliances, dishes, computer keyboards, glasses. This coursing energy: this really is something that happens to him. It takes him over, like a *dybbuk* or an *ibbur*. Eliezer is remembering a toy truck. There was something wrong with it—it wouldn't roll straight, or Eliezer had tripped on it—and he took the truck into his hands and smashed it on the floor, over and over again, until finally, a small plastic piece broke off. Small, but crucial, because now the truck wouldn't roll at all. It was junk. So Eliezer threw it against a wall, making a mark on the wall (for which he was spanked later) and then took it into his hands and broke it into small pieces. He was alive then, as now. He was made in God's image, capable of creation and destruction. If anger is idolatry, as the sages of blessed memory say, then who is the god it makes in its place?

When Eliezer and I first met, we were only just out of college, each in Israel on separate yeshiva programs. He had such a brilliant intensity, not like the boys I had dated in high school and college—wimpy, effeminate Modern Orthodox

dybbuk – spirit possession
ibbur – spirit incubation

boys with their thin-rimmed glasses and pale complexions. Eliezer was direct, serious, certain. He would quote Rav Kook, or Jabotinsky. He had so much vitality. And I knew that if I waited much longer, the quality of men would decrease. I wondered if his intensity would ever translate into cruelty. But the heart can deceive the mind when it wants enough.

Soon after we met, Eliezer and I went for a hike in the desert, down near Eilat, the red mountains, the open valleys dotted with acacia trees. We saw school groups hiking, singing. It was lovely, a taste of the world to come. Eliezer, his submachine gun banging against the side of his thigh, seemed jubilant. He said, if I remember correctly, "The most beautiful love isn't romantic love. 'Romantic'—it's an invention of the Romans. It's the love of our land, our people, and Hashem. This love is what unites us as Jews, it is *ahava* in its truest form."

At the time I found this inspiring. I was there but not there. And when we discovered that I could not bear children, I felt Eliezer's anger, for the first time, directed at me, even as he said outwardly that this was God's will, and that we would accept this decree. He even said to me, once, that since we were no longer fulfilling the mitzvah of *pru urvu*, that his only obligation was my pleasure.

But it seemed to me that without children, we had lost our sense of purpose. What was the point of this fruitless union? What was my purpose on Earth? Each of us coped

ahava – love
pru urvu – be fruitful and multiply

in different ways. I turned to spirituality. I went to see several tzaddikim, ostensibly for a *segulah* to help me become pregnant, but really, since I knew that was impossible, to taste the sparks of holiness that resided in these places. As a woman, many paths were closed to me, but these were open. And I discovered, by the graves of the rabbis, and in the courts of living miracle-workers, an entire world apart, filled with the scents of burning hyssop and incense, suffused with a kedusha that Eliezer's world scarcely knew. The women I met in these places taught me of the old ways, of herbs and amulets and secret things, of magical remedies and spells, incantations to attract angels and repel demons. It was astonishing to me, what could be permitted.

Eliezer filled the void with politics. He grew more and more resentful, enraged, and extreme. He met men who talked of war; he posted and commented and threatened people on the internet.

I replay what has just happened. There is Eliezer picking the television up from the table where it rested, swinging it around, not seeing me (or seeing me?), hitting me, knocking me down with such force, and then dropping it, shattering it. The sheer strength of him.

I hear Eliezer think: this is what happens when you love God too much. We should know better, but we are compelled, and we attract the nations' fury. Hashem yearns for us, and brings us to ruin.

I made excuses for him, right up until the end. "The frustration is more intense than you realize," I had said to my

segulah – amulet

mother only a few days ago. She lived in America. She was comfortable. "The world doesn't understand the threats we face."

"Tell her about the rockets!" Eliezer shouted from the other room.

"You know yesterday they found rockets," I said. "Just sitting there, in plain view. Who do we think these rockets are for? But does CNN report this? No. Nothing." My mother told me she was scared for us, that we should come back to Silver Spring, in America, that there were jobs there for Eliezer and we could see each other all the time.

"Is she trying to convince us to move back to America?" Eliezer shouted.

I feel myself leaving. I still hear Eliezer raging, justifying himself and what had happened, rehearsing what he would tell the police, then finally, dialing for help. But this is not the last thing I perceive.

I am at the mikva, about to immerse. But there is a creature in the mikva—a sort of manta ray, the sort of creeping, undulating thing that inhabits the floor of the ocean. I feel defiled, as if the creature's impurity has poisoned the mikva and infected me as well. I see the skull of a mouse that, when I was a little girl, I'd once found in the basement. I see the electric *ner tamid* flicker over the ark of my childhood shul. But these, too, are not the last things I perceive. Because now I smell incense from the *atzei shittim*, the acacia trees, rising in the crowded hall I once visited to receive blessings from a holy rebbetzin. It is a sweet smell, unlike any other. As the

ner tamid – eternal light

Torah hints, there is a secret ingredient in this incense, from the bark of the trees themselves, that can cause prophecy, and that the human brain itself produces at the moment of death. I feel it coursing through me. I know its provenance. And I see the manta ray in the mikva transform into a great snake, the *nachash* from Gan Eden, who opens Chava's eyes to the truth of the tree of knowledge. This snake is a woman, it is Chava's sister Lilit, it is the doorway to death, and I enter her and she enters me. And as this yichud takes place, I am no longer on the tile floor, I am a spark surrounded by thousands of others, reuniting with our source, a great, beautiful light that welcomes us. For a moment I wonder if I am worthy, if I must do tshuva to merit this dissolution, and I feel myself slip backward for a moment. But I am wrapped and held by the snake, which now is a woman, a womb and a death and a mother, saying only to me: Yes. And I see countless other worlds, and palaces, and the halls of polished stone, and I know there is nothing I need to say or do to be worthy, and with that I am enveloped in this *or ganuz*, this radiant and undying light, and I am dissolved into it, and I am no longer in that place but here in this one, and the acacia is within me and I am open and dissolved and here.

tshuva – repentance

THE SECRETS OF NAKEDNESS

1. ANDY, THE YOUNG LOVER WHO WANTS A SIMPLER LIFE

Here he is, Nathan thought: Andy, his beautiful, young lover, in bed with him in his Upper West Side apartment, light brown hair brushing against Nathan's naked chest. It was a moment filled with beauty: cold rain falling on Manhattan, a languorous Sunday morning in November. They had nowhere to go, nothing to do. And, Nathan knew, two years into a relationship, that they were fortunate and in love. Nathan looked down at Andy's smooth face; at twenty-five, his lover barely had to shave. Nathan felt lucky that such a beautiful young man was with him at this moment, and attending to him so devotedly.

Yet these very thoughts caused Nathan's arousal to subside, and so he quickly closed his eyes and summoned up images that, he knew, would bring himself to release. Nathan would do this often, even in his most passionate moments with Andy; it seemed as though no sensation or emotion could ever arouse Nathan as much as fantasies, some derived from pornography, some from memory, and others from pure imagination. Moreover, Nathan fantasized not about pleasure or intimacy, but about revelation; exposure; the dropping away of concealment. Nathan felt sure that Andy must know: must have noticed that his eyes were always closed as climax approached, must have felt that his mind was elsewhere. But maybe he didn't know? Many times, Nathan had thought of broaching the subject, confessing his secret, being more honest with this man he loved above all others. Was he afraid of hurting Andy, or of humiliating himself?

Andy. Just a week earlier, introducing him to some friends, Nathan felt a twinge at the diminutive, which only seemed to emphasize the nine-year difference in their ages. Nathan had thought that taking a younger lover would cause him to feel young again, but instead being with Andy reminded Nathan of how much a twenty-five-year-old he himself had remained, despite being thirty-four. His friends had suddenly grown up: one had been published in the *Times*, another was an award-winning architect, several had young children at home. They seemed on their way to somewhere. But Nathan had been out of law school for six years now and had held four different jobs. He dabbled in meditation, in writing, in the music he played on his guitar, alone, in his apartment. While his friends had focused their efforts and attained the early markers of success, Nathan seemed to drift like a child from curiosity to curiosity, flitting to the next one as soon as the novelty wore off. As a result, despite the difference in their ages, Nathan and Andy were at similar stages in their professional and personal lives. They both had promise, were both intelligent and thoughtful young men full of potential, except that Nathan had spent ten years not fulfilling it. More than once, Nathan had wondered if Andy, too, was merely another of these novelties, to be explored for a while but eventually left behind out of boredom. But no, Nathan told himself, that wasn't so; he loved Andy. The sex would work itself out. It wasn't the most important thing anyway.

There was an irony, too, in Nathan's absented lovemaking, which was that for the last two years, Nathan had practiced meditation under the guidance of an insightful and progressive rabbi named Susan Miller. Rabbi Miller had taught Nathan the value of mindfulness, of being present in the moment—and yet, here he was, on this lovely Sunday morning, deliberately losing himself in thought. So Nathan tried to focus, with an attention that would make Rabbi Miller proud, on the physical sensations of arousal itself. It worked, for a few moments—energy, tightness, excitement, pleasure—but then it didn't. So, almost as a reflex, his mind turned to naked bodies revealed in showers or doctor's offices or on beaches, and Nathan had his taste of bliss, and turned to reciprocate for his lover.

Afterward, Nathan and Andy lay in bed, idling. "I want to lead a simple life," Andy said. "I want to, I don't know, live in the country somewhere, and there'll be a little sign on a small road that says 'Jam,' and if you follow the sign, I'll be there and you can buy some jam."

"You'd have to sell a lot of jam," Nathan replied, staring at the off-white paint on the ceiling.

"Yeah, that's why it's a dream. But maybe someday."

"Maybe you'll marry a nice Jewish lawyer who can afford to buy the little country house for you." Nathan smiled.

"I don't know, where would I find someone like that?"

Andy asked playfully, and they returned to the embraces Nathan cherished more than sex.

Money. Another veil of separation, Nathan thought, like a *mechitza* between the two lovers. Nathan didn't mean to respond with dreadful practicality to Andy's innocent musings. But here he was, sounding like a much older man, maybe like his father. *You'd have to sell a lot of jam.* How deflating. But now Andy and I are in love, Nathan thought. We are in love, and it is true, and it was hard-fought. And who could argue, watching two young lovers cuddle in their bed, on a rainy autumn morning, in Manhattan, in an apartment they rented together, though with Nathan paying a somewhat larger share?

2. PETER AND SUSAN, NEITHER OF WHOM ASSUAGES NATHAN'S CONCERN

"Do you fantasize when you're with Carl?" Nathan asked Peter later that day, over Sunday brunch.

"Sometimes. Sometimes I take poppers."

Nathan had known Peter since college. When Nathan came out four years after graduation, Peter was one of the first people he told. Now he was a set designer, working on some well-reviewed off-Broadway production, and was a gay role model for Nathan, having maintained a relationship for many years—open, like everyone else's, but also with, it seemed, a real love between the two of them. Plus

mechitza – the partition between men and women in Orthodox synagogues

Peter seemed to have learned the secret arts of fashion, style, wit, and sensibility, which all gay men other than Nathan seemed somehow to possess.

"I think men fantasize," said Nathan, looking down at his fork. "It's the nature of the beast. Men are biologically wired for novelty, to spread our biological material over as wide a range as possible. Monogamy is a myth. Straight married men use porn and go to sex workers. Gay men aren't monogamous."

"Oh Nathan, your heteronormativity is showing!" Peter replied in a singsong way that still made Nathan wince. "Queers are different. We appreciate beauty—we appreciate it *too much*. We dress better, we look better, we decorate better. This isn't about evolution, honey, it's about *style*. If the straights had as much taste as we do, they'd be gay too."

Nathan had always thought Peter's flip demeanor concealed some sort of pain, a wound that lingered beneath the confidence. Nathan had never seen it expressed. But then again, had he asked?

"So, if it takes me so much beauty to get myself off that reality is never enough," said Nathan, "that's a *good* thing?"

"No Nathan, you're just a snob. Don't take yourself so seriously. Not everything has to be a good thing or a bad thing, it can just be a thing. A lovely, temporary thing. You don't have to understand it."

Nathan looked absently at the window. Unlike Peter, he had spent years in relationships with women. It was then that Nathan had learned to retreat into imagination, to bring to mind the exposure of a man's body, the first glimpse of the underlying nakedness, the secret that was no longer a secret. And now he could not unlearn it. Nathan drank from his cold glass of water and felt an ice cube tickle his lips.

That evening, before the meditation circle convened, Nathan confessed his problem to Rabbi Miller. They sat in her study, lined with books from floor to ceiling, a yoga mat rolled up and leaning against one of the shelves. Incense was burning, and Rabbi Miller looked serenely, yet fiercely, into Nathan's eyes. Nathan felt as if he were naked himself.

Nathan stammered for a while, and then said it: "When I am with my boyfriend, I am . . . distracted . . . by thoughts of other men. No, it's worse than that. I rely on those thoughts. To, you know. To, have an orgasm. I love Andy. I think. I don't know. I love holding Andy's body. But somehow—it's not enough. I want Andy to be enough. I feel dishonest."

Rabbi Miller looked into his eyes. She's straight, Nathan thought; no matter how open-minded she is, I bet she's repulsed. She is beautiful. Nathan fought the urge to look at her breasts.

"It is not your desire that is dishonest, Nathan," Rabbi Miller said. "That's just a desire. What is dishonest is your choice not to tell Andy."

"I couldn't."

"It's this fear that leads to dishonesty. Not the desire."

"But I feel so, I don't know, unspiritual. I'm supposed to be in the present moment, but when I'm with Andy, when I should be most present, I'm most absent."

There was a pause. Rabbi Miller, Nathan knew, would be happy to sit there in silence for an hour. Lapses in conversation were not awkward to her, with her eyes that could rest on anything, including your own, with a power that was no less terrifying for being quiet. To her, these unbearably awkward lacunae were merely pools of silence.

Finally, the rabbi stirred. "According to the Talmud, Nathan, there are three great kinds of secrets: the secrets of creation, which refer to science and everything about the world and how it operates; the secrets of the chariot, which refer to mysticism and everything about God; and the meaning of the laws of forbidden sexual relations—literally, *the secrets of nakedness.* What are the secrets of nakedness? And how are they connected to the others? What is the relationship between them?"

Another pause. "Maybe because sex and love are powerful?" Nathan offered. "Like how much of our lives are about love, and looking for it, or wanting it?"

"That could be," Rabbi Miller said, which Nathan understood to mean he was wrong. "The concealing of nakedness is also the veiling of the Divine reality, and at the same time, the expression of it. *Yesh* and *ayin*, being and nothingness, illusion and reality. Every plant stretching to the sun, every meal, every sexual encounter between humans, or animals, everything is suffused with eros. It is not the case that the material, the spiritual, and the sexual are so separate. Indeed, to know one, you must know all three."

"But how do I do that?" Nathan asked.

"You know, Nathan," Rabbi Miller said, somehow appearing to sit back even more in her chair, "the Maggid of Mezritch, one of the great Hasidic teachers, had a practice for unwanted thoughts that would come to him during prayer. The traditional way to rid oneself of these distractions was to push them out of the mind. If you thought of a beautiful woman, or I suppose, a beautiful man, you would imagine him or her dead and buried, with worms crawling in and out of her flesh. Something awful, to realize that beauty is transitory, and thus unworthy of our attention."

"Okay," said Nathan.

"But, based on the teachings of his master the Baal Shem Tov, the Maggid had a different approach. He would take each thought to its root. If the Maggid thought of a beautiful woman, he would say to himself, 'What do I desire about this woman? Her beauty?' And the Maggid would focus on the aspect of God that was the source of beauty, the sefirah of *tiferet*. Likewise if he was thinking of money, he might ponder why he was thinking of money, and realize that it was to keep his wife happy, which came from the root of *netzach*—sustainability, endurance. Or if it was someone who had done him wrong, he would think of justice and of forgiveness. In so doing, he would elevate each thought to its source, and every source was an emanation of God."

"So what do I do?"

"You must do the same, Nathan," answered Rabbi Miller, scratching behind her left ear. "The Kabbalists understood the hidden shape of the cosmos to be the body of the *Adam Kadmon*, the primordial human. They even measured it, scandalously to some, dimension by dimension. Perhaps

tiferet – a Kabbalistic sefirah that integrates *hesed* (lovingkindness) and *gevurah* (strength)

you, too, are attempting to uncover that which has been concealed. Explore these thoughts of fantasy, and take them to their root. Let them enter you, and inquire into their source. Practice what the Maggid advised, and then let's talk more."

That evening, as the group sat in meditation, Nathan did as he had been instructed, allowing his mind to wander to the erotic images that aroused him the most. But what he saw troubled him. Though he had never noticed it before, Nathan observed that the images he most regularly summoned were not of intimacy or consummation, not of climax or embrace, but of exposure: of men being stripped (in a locker room, fraternity house, massage studio, class-room), of incidental contacts turning into more, of naked-ness and its uncovering. Even the act of undressing, Nathan found, was eroticized, as it came to represent a kind of laying-bare: there he is, for all to see. Nathan was startled that he had never noticed it before. If this was the body of God, it was God in the form of a satyr, nudity suddenly revealed. What was the "root" of this?

3. ALAN, A STRANGER WHO PROPOSES A SOLUTION

The bell chimed, ending the meditation session.

"Now I'd like you to find a partner," Rabbi Miller said, in her soft "meditation" voice, "preferably someone you haven't partnered with before, and dialogue for a few minutes about whatever arose for you in the last sit."

Nathan felt terrified—and betrayed: How could Rabbi Miller invite him to ponder his fantasies, knowing full well that he would then be asked to share them with another? Nathan looked around the room. There were only eight people—it wasn't as if he could sneak off without anyone noticing. Rabbi Miller sat at the front of the room—somehow, the circle did have a front, and she was undoubtedly it, with her yogi clothes and meditation chimes, the composed expression on her face. To her right was Denise ("I prefer to be called Bracha") Gottschalk, who was very proud that Nathan was her "gay friend," and who showered him in endless, banal confidences—"Isn't he the hottest?" "I just *have* to get a pedicure." Nathan was relieved that Denise had already paired off with Reuven, a retired professor in his seventies. Next to Denise were two people Nathan didn't know talking with two others he wanted to avoid. There was only one person left: a man a bit older than Nathan, with a thick black beard. The man looked over and stood up.

Too late now, Nathan thought.

"I'm Alon," said the man, walking up. "But I go by Alan."

"Nathan. Are you new here?"

"I just moved here from Boston. I was born in Israel." Sitting down. Rearranging.

"Oh wow," said Nathan. "What do you do?"

"I'm a child psychiatrist. Should we get started?" The man was direct.

"Sure. Why don't you go first?"

Alan gave an unremarkable report. He described how his

back had begun to hurt twenty minutes in; how the pain felt; how he let it progress rather than shift positions. Nathan felt sweat drip from under his arms, and offered helpful, banal suggestions.

"So now it's your turn."

There is something about sitting in silence with another person, Nathan thought, that creates a bond where there shouldn't be one. At least half is projection. But maybe only half. Maybe there is also a real closeness that comes from the clothing of words being shed. So. Deep breath.

"Yeah," Nathan answered. "It's hard, I guess. Because Susan gave me some specific instructions, which were . . . difficult."

"Okay." Alan didn't vary his gaze.

"Well. Huh. Okay, well, I'm gay, first of all." No response. "I was in the closet for a long time, but I've been out for a few years. I'm seeing this wonderful guy right now. But—whoo, this is hard—what I was talking to Susan about was, I've been getting . . . distracted . . . I guess . . . during . . . sex. Not like thoughts that come in unwanted, I mean, I spoke to Susan because—I invite them in—in order to—well—be satisfied. I think these thoughts more than I think of Andy. The guy I'm seeing. And, it's hard, because, I don't really—I want to be with Andy. I don't want to have these thoughts the way I have them. I want to have sex with someone, you know, and not be unfaithful. Because I feel unfaithful, when I'm with him but thinking about someone else. Even if it's an imaginary someone else. And, like, a hypocrite, because of mindfulness; it's supposedly like, be in the present moment, but I'm always flying off into fantasy. So, I asked Susan about what to do."

"Okay," Alan said.

Was he not going to respond, ever? Nathan felt under attack, simply because Alan had said nothing. Alan, or Alon? He didn't even commit to a name. But now it was too late to retreat. Nathan took another deep breath, felt the heat of his blushing, and blushed more at having blushed.

"So, Susan had me, or asked me to think about, these thoughts that I get, or these images, you know, or— sometimes they're not even images, sometimes it's just a phrase, like 'There he is' or something like that, you know, about someone who I might've seen like one time in a shower, or something—and I was supposed to think slowly of one of these things and allow the thought to go wherever it would go, and notice it. And try to see the 'root' of the thought, you know, where it comes from, what it really is. So, I did. It was hard. I mean, it felt kind of intimate. Or inappropriate, even. Like it didn't belong here. So, that's kind of what I was doing for most of the sit."

"What did you think about?"

"Well, I don't know if you want to hear that!" Nathan said with a false joviality.

But Alan made no response, only looked at him still with penetrating eyes—not unlike Rabbi Miller's from a short time ago, Nathan thought. Nathan could not articulate why he felt moved to continue, but he did, feeling a bit like he was falling.

"Well, okay, so, sure," he started, "so, I thought about

what images really are the ones that recur. You know, it's not like I always search for one or another. But a couple come back more than others. Like I said. Men in showers, maybe a little younger than me, men who aren't exposing themselves, but who are exposed anyway. The, uh, penis . . . like, as if it were a secret that was unwittingly shared. Are you sure it's okay to say all this stuff? It feels, like, inappropriate or not okay."

"Thanks for asking," replied Alan with an unsettling confidence. "It's okay with me if it's okay with you."

"Okay, well, stop me at any point. So, right, maybe men having to get naked for a medical exam or in a locker room, or, I don't know. I think it's—it's not the sex, that's not the part that is exciting. It's the exposure. That's what I saw in the sit. That it was that moment of . . . revelation, almost. But nothing came up around 'what is this about?' What is its 'root,' you know? So I feel more confused than before. I get that it's the moment of revealing, like, getting naked, but I don't know, is that like a fetish or something? Or maybe something from my past? It's like, intimacy in one sense but also the opposite of intimacy. It makes me feel broken."

Nathan paused, waiting for a reply, but then Rabbi Miller called the group back together, and for a few minutes, some of the participants shared what they had learned. Eventually, she sounded the bell once again and the group began to disperse.

"Thanks for listening, I guess," Nathan said to Alan.

"Would you like to continue?"

"What?"

"You were interrupted. Would you like to continue, after the class is over?"

Of course it sounds like a pickup line, Nathan thought. So *that's* how it is. Oh, well that's kind of hot.

"Well," Nathan laughed feebly, "you're not *my* shrink. I wouldn't feel right."

"I don't mind. I don't have anything to do now. Like I said, I'm kind of new here. I appreciate your openness; it's refreshing. And if I can help you, I'd like to do that."

Nathan looked into Alan's eyes, which once again reminded him of Susan's.

"How?"

"We could sit at a café. But my apartment is also just two blocks away, and it would be quieter. We can just walk over."

"Really?" Nathan said, thinking, okay, definitely, this is what I think it is. Or is it? "Okay. I mean, if it's not any trouble."

"Not at all. I value the connection. I'm not your therapist, just a friend."

Nathan followed Alan out of the room, and they put on their shoes in the hall. Alan had nice shoes, Nathan noticed: brown casual shoes. But not particularly stylish. Could go either way, gay or not. The beard was trimmed, but not too short. Still not quite sure.

"Are you sure this is okay?" Nathan asked, as they walked outside.

"Yes."

"Okay," Nathan said. But again he felt unsure. Was Alan trying to seduce him? Isn't this . . . weird? But is he, even?

What is "gaydar" anyway? More concealment. Nathan thought of asking outright. He wanted to make it clear that he wasn't going to Alan's apartment for sex. But then, is that even true—I mean, it's hot to think about, Nathan thought, I am open to it. No, he continued, I better not ask, because I'm probably the only one thinking of sex, and how embarrassing it would be to say something and be exposed as the one thinking about sex, when obviously this is not about sex—right? Like then I'm the pervert. Emotional intimacy can feel like sex, Nathan thought, the awkwardness and the nakedness, but it's not sex. Right?

So Nathan stayed quiet for the entire two-minute walk. A light rain was falling, a mist really, so neither Alan nor Nathan opened their umbrellas.

Finally they arrived at the ground floor of a brownstone and entered the building. Though he had said he'd only just moved in, Alan did not hesitate with the keys or the door handles, did not betray any sense of uncertainty. Nor, when they reached it, was Alan's apartment filled with boxes; it was sparely, even serenely, decorated: a few bookshelves (Nathan scanned for familiar spiritual books, and saw a few, together with psychology texts and novels he hadn't heard of) with a few small bowls resting on them, a Japanese painting on one of the walls, two small sofas across from each other in the living room. Nathan felt inadequate—his own apartment was a cluttered mess. What am I doing here? He thought. Is this even for real? Are we about to hook up? Nathan thought he should take off his shoes. He watched Alan to see if he'd remove his. He didn't. So Nathan didn't either. They walked in and sat on the opposite sofas.

Another awkward silence. "I'm feeling a little anxious," Nathan said. He crossed and uncrossed his legs.

"That's understandable. What would help you feel at ease?"

"I'm worried that you want to have sex with me," Nathan blurted out.

"Why are you worried about that?"

"Because that's not why I'm here. I don't want you to get the wrong idea, to think I'm that kind of person." Nathan paused. "I mean, I am that kind of person, but not if that's not what you want, and it's fine if you don't, but I'm not sure. I don't want to be . . . invasive."

"It's good that you are concerned about my feelings. Isn't it?"

Nathan thought for a moment. "Yes, I guess so," he said. Still no confirmation.

Alan said, without a pause, "You were saying how you are troubled by needing fantasies to attain orgasm."

"Yes," Nathan said. "But I don't really know what else to tell you."

"It's not that uncommon. Men fantasize all the time."

"But I feel like I do it *all* the time."

"It sounds like you're in a lot of pain."

"I guess I am." Nathan felt himself choking up involuntarily. This was not what he wanted. "I'm afraid of being lonely again. I hate it. I can take being a failure. But I can't take being lonely like that again, like I was for so long. Andy's wonderful. He's beautiful, he really is. He's smarter than he seems." It occurred to Nathan that Alan had never met Andy, had no opinion of how he seemed. "I mean, he comes off as being sort of—I don't know—not dumb, not at all, but just—I don't know, normal. But he's really wonderful. I used to think that love would solve every problem, that people in love had no idea how lucky they were. They forgot. Forgot what it meant to be alone. But now that I'm one of those people, I still feel like there's this distance between me and them. That I'll never be okay."

"That must really hurt."

"But the fantasies, that's the point—they aren't really fantasies of other men. They're fantasies of situations. It's not about who is getting naked, or even what they look like, it's *a guy that's naked*. A guy that shouldn't be naked. Or, a guy who's about to be. I mean—the point is, it's not like I imagine any particular person."

But as Nathan spoke, he was thinking, over and over again: What am I doing here?

"Was there ever a time when you felt that way?" Alan asked.

"What?"

"Naked," Alan said. "Exposed unwillingly."

"I don't know. Sometimes I think that I was abused, or something, as a child, when I was young. But I don't—I don't have any memory of it at all, nothing. Not even a flash of something. Just, being naked, sure, with my father, going to the bathroom. Flushing the toilet. Him showing me how. But that's not abuse—that's, I don't know if it means anything. I don't think it does. I don't think that everything has to stand for something. It doesn't."

"So what does it mean, then?"

"I think that the value of the secret is that it's a secret, not meant to be shared openly."

"And when it is shared openly—"

"That's what's hot. Revelation. It's not like, oh this guy's got a big dick, or, look, this guy's got chest hair, or whatever. The details don't matter. It's just that first there was a secret, and now everything is exposed."

"So what arouses you is the truth."

Nathan laughed. "You know, in the meditation I thought a little about the Adam Kadmon, you know, the primordial man or whatever, the Kabbalistic idea, and I thought that maybe there's sort of a primordial—that this is a kind of knowledge. That it's spiritual, not only sexual. But then I thought, what if the spiritual is only the sexual projected upward in the mind? You know, like Freud. Like it's just sublimated sex in the end."

"Or maybe it's the opposite," said Alan. "Maybe the sexual is a metaphor for the spiritual. Maybe sex is how it's expressed on one level, and the spiritual is how it's expressed on another."

"But I don't feel liberated, I feel stuck," said Nathan.

"So strip right now."

"What?"

"If nakedness is a metaphor, then do it right now."

Nathan sat perfectly still and looked into Alan's eyes again. So this *was* what he had been after all along! Well that makes it simple, thought Nathan, now it's just hot. But wait, does he? How far is it even possible to go not knowing whether something is sex or not? But this was his fantasy, after all, and now it was here. Should I do it? Nathan asked himself. He felt as if afloat. Yes. He kept his eyes fixed on Alan's as he took off his shirt and put it beside him on the sofa. When he took off his shoes, he had to break his gaze for a moment when one of them wouldn't come untied, and at that moment he felt doubt, but as soon as he looked back at Alan, he continued, and took off his socks. He unbuckled his belt and unbuttoned his jeans, stood up, and pulled down his pants and underwear together, his erection pointing straight out from his body. Alan stood up opposite him, still fully clothed and looking only into Nathan's eyes.

"Are you aroused now?" Alan asked, their eyes still locked together.

"Obviously."

"Why?"

"Because I shouldn't be naked now, but I am. Because this shouldn't be happening."

"Do you think I know more about you, now that you are naked?"

"Yes. I do." Nathan got harder.

"Even saying it makes you more aroused."

"Yes."

"And hearing me talk about it."

"Yes, yes."

"Do you want to touch yourself?"

"Yes," Nathan almost panted.

"Do you want *me* to touch it?"

"It doesn't matter."

"It doesn't matter?"

"Because, I'm naked—"

"Are you attracted to me?" Alan asked.

"Not really. You're . . . not my type."

"What in particular?"

"The beard, the . . . I don't know, you're older than me. I like them young, I guess. It's a cliché."

"You don't think it's more than that?"

"I don't know."

"Did you ever think, Nathan, of who it is in those images?"

"What do you mean."

"Who is it that is exposed, in the gym or the doctor's office—who is that person?"

"I don't know, just—I don't know—"

"You do know."

"It's me."

"It's you, Nathan, exposed as you are now. Your fantasies aren't of other men. They're of you. There are no other men."

"Y-you don't want to touch me?"

"Who are you, now, naked here, in front of me?"

"I feel like a child."

"And how does that feel?"

"I don't know. I—I feel scared. I feel like you could do anything you wanted. But I also—I also feel free."

"That's right, say more about that."

"I feel, there's nothing left to hide, this is all there is, my body, this is who I am, the failure, the faggot, the, well, this is my body, for better or worse, this is who I am." Nathan sobbed, but continued. "But that's fine. That's fine. It's better than the hiding, all the time, the constant pretending, the clothing, the being a man and knowing what to do and how I'm supposed to live, when actually I have no idea."

There was a pause. The air felt cold against Nathan's body. He was no longer aroused and yet felt somehow more aroused, as if on fire.

"Nathan, there is nothing else, there is no door you stand outside of, nothing you don't know. You are okay, Nathan." Alan reached over and placed his arms around Nathan's shoulders, and rested Nathan's head on them.

Nathan wept fully now. "I never know. There are people who know, and I never know. I want life to begin. All my friends have . . . but I'm so . . . stunted. I'm never ready. I want there to be something more, something—like when I met Rabbi Miller, I felt it, like . . . like this was God, enlightenment. But when I let go into that, I get . . . edgy. Like there was a kind of synchronicity that's terrifying, like the world doesn't exist at all and is only in my mind. Like I could go insane if I let myself believe it. As if, everything is just sending me signs to—"

"Wake up."

Nathan took his head off Alan's shoulders. Now he desperately wanted Alan to touch him, to take him back to what he knew, to a story of seduction. Anything but here, in this—place, in this place without roots, but with wheels within wheels and the sound of rushing waves.

"You *are* being dreamt, Nathan. What is this exposure

that you yearn for, that you yearn to be revealed? To finally relinquish this illusion, that you are a wave distinct from the sea. Take it to its root, Nathan. You and I are characters in a story, but one with no author and no reader, only the story reading itself, with no inside and no outside. There is no greater intimacy than this, Nathan. The secret you want to know is not a secret. It is already naked, already revealed."

"No!" Nathan suddenly shouted. He put his hands inside Alan's shirt, and started furiously to open it, stumbling over the buttons. "No, no, no."

Alan stood still, allowing but not encouraging. He was sturdily built—an oak, like his original name. His chest was hairy. "Nathan, you don't want to see me. You want to see yourself. Look into my eyes," said Alan, as Nathan fell still.

"This is what you want," Alan continued. "This is the root of sex, Nathan: to look into the eyes of the lover and see yourself looking back. *Sitrei arayot, ma'aseh merkavah.* Religion isn't sublimated sex. Sex is sublimated religion."

"But—" Nathan began.

"I am here and you are there, but there is also a way to see only the words on this page, the letters of creation assembling and disassembling. This is the root of the unconcealing, this knowing, which you have always known, and this aching at the pain of it. Can you feel it, as your eyes look into mine?"

sitrei arayot – laws of forbidden relations (lit. "the concealments/secrets of nakedness")
ma'aseh merkavah – early form of Jewish mysticism (lit. "workings of the chariot")

"I . . . y-yes."

"And this is also the root of union, Nathan, that I am here with you at your most intimate. Let me inside you, Nathan. I want to see you dissolve in my eyes, like a lover's in ecstasy, and me in yours, both of us dreams, characters, appearances."

Nathan was silent.

"You know, Nathan, that there is a knowing inside you that this is real, this truth, this God, this way of knowing; whatever it is; this, Nathan the prophet, is what you seek to unclothe."

And as Nathan stood there, his heart and skin as if on fire, Alan gently took his face into his hands, and finally kissed him lightly on the lips, and it was as the holy books say, *he died with a kiss*, and it was in just this way that Nathan, for a moment, did die, and knew the great peace of relinquishment.

THE ACACIA TREE

I invite you to imagine a girl, a young woman, named Yonit. She has recently celebrated her sixteenth birthday in Jerusalem, where her parents immigrated and settled just before she was born. Her family is religious, but modern. They speak English in their four-room apartment, although they often switch without thinking into Hebrew when the words of their former language suddenly seem to fail. Yonit's brown hair is long and tied back. She is politically centrist. She is headstrong, intelligent, and musical.

Yonit's closest friends are other children of Anglo *oleh* families. Tamar's parents came from Chicago back in the eighties; Rachel's from England, only ten years ago—she still has memories of Marmite and Hobnobs, and of streets with brick-clad semidetached houses stretching across North London. All the girls speak Hebrew to one another—they are Israelis, and blend effortlessly with everyone in school, even some of the Sephardic and Mizrahi girls. But when it is late at night and they want to talk intimately about boys or parents or music, they cleave, as it were, to their own kind.

Yonit's parents were conflicted as to how best to educate their daughter. In Israel, the Jewish school system is segregated between religious and secular, with only a few institutions offering something between traditional Orthodox observance and nothing at all. The Friedmans had been liberal American Jews. They kept the mitzvot, the Sabbath especially, and knew they wanted their children—Yonit, her younger brother Avi, and her baby sister Margalit—to learn Torah as well as secular studies. But the first religious principal who met with the Friedmans to discuss their children winked at Yonit's father and said that, in his opinion, women who learn Talmud grow up to disobey their husbands.

So Yonit was sent to as left-leaning a religious school as the Friedmans could find, with the result being that Yonit, at the age of her bat mitzvah, complained that the "real religious kids" were learning more than she was, and couldn't she switch to the *dati* school, where even if she couldn't learn Gemara she could at least learn what she did learn more seriously, with more devotion and intensity. Some of the other girls at shul, Yonit said, could already tell her how to comb her hair on Shabbat; could recite *mishnayot* by heart; could, and this seemed most important, claim a personal relationship with God. The Friedmans were ambivalent at first, especially Batsheva, Yonit's mother, but eventually a suitable religious school was found, and Yonit's friend Tamar Menashe went there already, so Yonit went to find her relationship with God the "real" way. The piety of the religious girls—this almost instinctual assumption on their part that God is present in their lives—this is what Yonit wants.

dati – religious
mishnayot – passages of the Mishnah

One of Yonit's most treasured memories is when, a little over a year ago, just as the flowers were beginning to bloom in the Jerusalem hills, she and Tamar and Rachel hiked with some of Tamar's religious friends to one of the natural springs outside the city and played guitar and sang songs by Shlomo Carlebach. Yonit loved her friends' effortless spirituality, felt at the spring a sense of naturalness, ease, and comfort—not just with God, but with the holy land and nature, all of which were bound together with love. Tamar, Rachel, and their friends seemed to her to be *in place*, at ease with their context and people and land, whereas she, Yonit, seemed still to have to earn the love of God.

"I wonder sometimes about how I relate to Hashem," Yonit tells Rachel in Hebrew, one long and lazy Shabbat afternoon.

"What do you mean?"

"I feel like I'm always testing Him, as if, I'm always, *k'ilu*, saying, 'Okay, Hashem, if you'll grant me this one favor, I'll believe in you and know you exist.'"

"But if you're always testing from the outside, you'll never know. Because you have to know from the inside," Rachel answers.

"I know. That's what I'm saying," Yonit continues. "I have the *emunah*, and I feel it when I'm learning or praying. But then other times I wonder if my emunah is real. I wish one time maybe Hashem would test me instead of the other way around."

k'ilu – like
emunah – faith

"Don't wish for such a thing! What are you saying, Yonit? Don't wish for God to test you in any way. Be happy that God *doesn't* test you like He tested Avraham or Iyyov. So maybe you would pass, Baruch Hashem, great for you. But whether you would pass or fail is not the point. The point is that you should never have to suffer in this way."

"Still, isn't it true that when you love someone, you want to prove it?"

"If David Pereg wanted me to prove it, he wouldn't have to test me!" Rachel laughs and throws a piece of chocolate.

David Pereg is seventeen, one of the best-looking, coolest, and most respected boys in the school. All the girls idolize him—even those who don't, pretend to do so out of a desire to belong—and all the boys follow his lead. One day he came to school with a new kippah, with a kind of multicolored ring design. A week later, half the boys in his class (and most of the ones below it) had similar ones.

A year earlier, Yonit had met David Pereg one time in the street, walking home after a few hours she'd spent reading in a meadow. "Shalom, Yonit," David had said. It was the first time they had ever spoken. To be spoken to by David Pereg!

"Hi, David."

"How are you?"

"Baruch Hashem. And you?"

"Ah, okay, I guess."

Yonit did not know how to answer. What was next to say? Why did he only "guess" he was okay? Was this a new thing—to be not so sure one was okay? Or did he mean it? Could it be that David Pereg wanted to confide in her, to talk to her in a way that boys never wanted to talk to her? David Pereg? Of all people? He could have answered that he was "fine," that everything was *b'seder*—why this act of self-revelation?

Then again, Yonit thought, he hasn't said anything yet, only that he might want to say.

To tell the truth, Yonit does not share her classmates' enthusiasm for David Pereg. He seems to her too confident— he and his crowd always parade through the school halls as if they own the place. But Yonit feels that she can see through them. They are petrified of the army, she thinks. Today they are carousing in the schoolyard, calling each other names, but in one or two years they could be in some refugee camp, shooting at people. They act as though their youth is never going to end, because unlike Yonit's American cousins, they know it will end, very definitely and very soon.

Yonit wishes that she could connect with the boys on this more honest level. She wants to know them in a real way, without every statement being taken as some sort of innuendo. But with boys like David, the ground rules are established. He knows that every girl wants to kiss him, to be with him; he knows how to behave around the boys; and so there is no undoing his personality, no getting beneath the mask.

The fault, Yonit thinks, lies not with the boys but with the girls, who divide neatly into two distinct camps. The first, the good girls, will not so much as kiss a boy, and everyone knows it. For all Rachel's boasting, she would never "prove her love" for David Pereg, even if given the chance. She is not *shomeret n'giah* exactly; she might hold hands with a boy. But if David Pereg wanted the kind of "proof" that only a woman could offer him, Rachel would not be amenable.

The other girls, of course, are the bad girls. These girls are indistinguishable from the good girls in appearance, speech, and attitude, but somehow word got around that they would do anything, or anything short of *that* thing, with almost anyone. Shlomit Hazony, for example. No one really knew for sure if she had been with David Pereg himself, but everyone knew for sure that she had been with every other boy in his crowd: David Berger, Itzik Heiligman, Ofer Oz. Everyone knew because she talked. She talked about how Itzik was bigger than Ofer, but Ofer came faster. How one time Mr. Sofer, the math teacher, had a hard-on when he had to talk to her after class, and how she saw him trying to glimpse her cleavage. Shlomit talked, never to a group of more than one or two others, but always to the right people so that word got around; so that the boys, too, knew, and so that if they saw *her* alone on the street, they would know their opportunity.

Yonit thinks of herself as neither a good girl nor a bad girl. As a matter of reality, of what she has done and has not done, she is a good girl—but not out of ideology. For a few weeks, she'd "dated" a Moroccan boy named Amir Paz, who she thought might reach over and kiss her one time, because it was said that Moroccan Jews were more liberal about these things. But Amir never made a move, and Yonit quickly grew to find him boring. So Yonit gained the reputation

---

shomer or *shomeret n'giah* – observant of chastity laws

of a good girl, and now few of the boys regard her with any interest. She is attractive, Yonit's friends all say; as Rachel once said to her (to widespread laughter) "Your breasts are definitely a presence." She has lovely brown hair, even has a pretty laugh, if such a thing can really be described. But a good girl simply does not draw much interest.

And yet why this dichotomy? It's not natural, Yonit thinks. Why the choice between A or B, red or white? Surely there must be some boys at school like her, boys who would like to . . . explore, neither remaining so chaste that nothing could ever happen, nor acting so sex-crazed that everything happens at once. After all, doesn't the Gemara teach of sex that "this, too, is Torah?" Yonit remembers the story well: R. Kahana hides under Rav's bed to learn the secrets of sex —and criticizes his methods no less!—defending his actions because sex, too, is part of the life of Torah. How the girls laughed when they learned that one. And yet, in real life, it's as if one has to choose a team.

Yonit prefers the quiet boys in her class, not the David Peregs of the world, but the young scholar who writes poetry, the sensitive boy, the shy one. She imagines intimate conversations on the telephone, at first, followed by discreet meetings in fields—always outdoors, not in cafés. The first kiss happens on a warm day in the park. Later, days later, they meet again, but this time it is somewhere private, and Yonit reaches her hand under his shirt, the scholar's, and feels his nipples hard under his tzitzis. He is emboldened, reaches out his hand, and, with a gasp, touches her breast.

tzitzis – fringes/fringed undergarment

They kiss again. Yonit reaches down her hand to feel him through his jeans, and he gasps again. No one has ever touched him there. He kisses her neck. All is gentle, slow, and quiet.

So when David Pereg had stopped on the street—*stopped* on the street, Yonit realized; they were not even walking anymore; they were definitely stopped and talking—Yonit had not known what to do. David confessed to being okay, he *guessed*, in such a tone as to invite the obvious next question. And Yonit, after a moment's thought, decided to ask it:

"Why only 'you guess'?"

I invite you to imagine, for a moment, which answer you would most like to hear. Is it that David Pereg is a sensitive boy after all, that under his arrestingly beautiful looks there is a soul that recognizes in Yonit a fellow traveler, a fellow poet under the stars? Shall he confess, then, to his fears or anxieties? Or perhaps he seduces Yonit with a mere presentation of vulnerability, eventually inviting her back to his apartment (his parents are gone for the day to visit relatives in Netanya) where he will show her a passion that she does not even know she longs for? Or: perhaps you might like David to say something banal (perhaps even vulgar) that reassures Yonit she is right to shun boys like him and favor the quiet, anonymous scholar.

We can invent this past because, a year later, Yonit has completely forgotten whatever David had said, so inconsequential was his reply. She was flustered, that is what she remembers. She thinks: I was only fifteen then, a child. In any case, her encounter with David Pereg did not lead to erotic passion or emotional connection. It led to nothing. Then again, who knows what might have happened, had she probed a little more, exposed herself to risk and love and pain?

But now Yonit finds Rachel's invocation of David Pereg annoying. She says so. "We're not talking about David Pereg, we're talking about Hashem."

"Is there a difference?" Rachel continues to joke.

"Seriously!"

"Yonit: let me tell you something," Rachel says. "Stop thinking so much. I don't mean you should be an idiot. I mean about Hashem. Stop thinking so much and you'll feel Him. It's that simple. The mind gets in the way of the heart. I don't analyze my relationship with Hashem all the time. It is part of life, that is all. Do you think of your relationship to the air all the time? What is important is to breathe. Do you understand?"

"But air is proven. We know it is there, because we breathe it every day."

"Faith means that God is proven too, and you know it, because you are with Him every day also."

"I—"

"Look at this plant, Yonit. See how it is breathing? Because God created it this way. See how the breeze blows? Because God wants it to."

"But," Yonit replied, "it could also be said that the plant evolved this way and the wind is how it is because of whatever scientific cause there is for the wind."

"I know that, Yonit. It's a question of how we understand it. It's not something you can think. You feel it, you understand it. You have to stop thinking so much," Rachel concludes.

Yonit is dissatisfied with this answer, but this time she does not tell Rachel so. What the conversation has revealed is not anything about God but something about the gap growing between Yonit and Rachel.

* * *

As a religious girl growing up in Israel, Yonit has taken dozens, if not hundreds, of hikes throughout the country. This is part of the Israeli educational system, hearkening back to the pioneering days when knowing the land was part of what every *chalutz* should know. Yonit has visited wadis, springs, canyons, mountains, caves, lakes, forests, deserts, seas, rivers, foothills, ruins, villages, archeological digs, cisterns, churches, synagogues, fortresses, graves, tombs, and monasteries. She knows the difference between Mamluk and Crusader architecture, between the Syrian-African rift and the Carmel, between the Judean desert and the Negev. And Yonit loves these trips, loves learning about almond trees and hyssop and which flowers can make good tea. While many of her friends complain about marching over the Judean hills in long skirts and sneakers, Yonit feels at one with the natural world, even in such a state. Particularly in such a state—her very body dressed in a way that relates to God, her soul singing songs in the world God created.

chalutz – pioneer

Yonit has loved these trips so much that she yearns to take one on her own. On field trips, everyone talks endlessly about nothing. Once, her class was hiking up Mount Meron, in the Galilee, where Rabbi Shimon Bar Yochai is buried and where the Kabbalah was born, and her friends were talking about television shows! About their favorite videos online! In the shadow of the grave of the tzaddik! Yonit knew better than to try to demand respect for the holiness of the sacred site, so she hung back, trudging along with the slower-moving kids who were usually too exhausted by huffing and puffing to speak. Even then, Rachel called out, "Where is Yonit?" and teased her for walking slowly. It would be better to explore alone, Yonit thinks, yet she knows this is an impossibility. Her parents would never allow it—unescorted girls, with no security guard, wandering through mountains? Impossible to conceive—which threat was worse, the boys or the terrain or the Arabs or the thieves? But every day of Yonit's life is watched, planned, supervised. If she is not in school, she is with her family. Ah, to break free!

It is the desert that beckons the most. The quiet and the space—it seemed to Yonit on her class trip to the Negev, which lasted almost a full week, that God's voice could be heard there more clearly than anywhere else. Indeed, upon her return, Yonit had to cover her ears from the constant noise, the traffic, the refrigerator humming, the toilets flushing, the sirens blaring as police cars raced across Jerusalem. How she wished she was back among the silent, tan mountains, with nothing but the occasional jet plane overhead and not even the chirping of birds to shatter the silence. The walls of Jerusalem increasingly grew to look like those of a prison. What had previously delighted Yonit—walks in the park, playing with Margalit, good books—came to feel like the gilding on a cage. Now Yonit contemplates her well-ordered life and, as she comes to consider it, despairs. After this will come the army, and then college, and then marriage— when will she ever be able to be alone, herself, just her and Hashem, with as much time and space as she wants?

And then, just after Pesach, an opportunity arises: a June service project, advertised at her school, on a kibbutz not far from Eilat, at the southern tip of the Negev. She knows that none of her friends will want to do it, working in the desert in the heat. And so she signs up—sure enough, the only one in her circle who does. Her family approves; they're delight- ed that she's donating her time and labor in this way. But Yonit decides to deploy a stratagem. On the last day of the program, she will take a day for herself instead of returning straight home, and hike in the mountains near Eilat. She will seek the intimacy of Hashem in the quiet of the desert and still be back in Jerusalem before midnight. And she will at last be alone.

As the days of the Omer tick by and Shavuot approaches, Yonit becomes enflamed with excitement, and nervousness, and doubt. Will someone find out? She has covered every track. Is it right to deceive her friends and her family in this way? But otherwise she will never do it. And her motive is pure, and the fruits of a pure motive are pure, she tells

Pesach – Passover

herself. Yonit sneaks over to the Society for the Protection of Nature in Israel shop downtown, buys trail maps and guides to hiking in the Negev, reads all she will need to do to prepare. She already knows how to stay safe, what one needs to survive, what to do and what she needs. She tells no one. It's like she is plotting a sort of coup. But her motives come from God.

So, after just a few weeks, Yonit finds herself on a bus to Eilat, where she will catch another one to the small kibbutz where the program is based. Inside her backpack are maps and hiking boots, water bottles and protective gear. Now she is alone on the bus, in a sort of prelude, she imagines, to the sweet solitude to come.

Yonit has never wished to be secular, ever. She sees the *hilonim*'s lives as spiritually empty, and sees their culture as constantly compensating for this void with shopping malls and fashion and loud, cheap music. But on the bus to Beer-sheva, Yonit looks at a woman sitting two rows ahead, with short-cropped hair and a sense of ease emanating from her, and begins to think: What would it be like? To be so free? To have no sense of obligation, no limits? This woman—she seems so composed. She is calm, Yonit thinks. I am masquerading on this short vacation, but for her, is life always this free?

All continues according to plan. The work is tedious, but the time passes quickly, and she talks each day with her friends and her parents on the phone. Finally, on the last day, Yonit rises at sunrise, quickly davens shacharit—adding extra tehillim to apologize for this small deception in the name of *ahavat hashem*—and, as arranged, takes an early bus to the Eilat central bus station. It is ironic, Yonit thinks: to be in the sacred space of the desert I must first traverse this strange city of vulgarity and noise, filled with tourists getting drunk and burning their bodies on the beach. It is the shell before the fruit, Yonit tells herself; the husk around the seed. Yonit stores her baggage at the bus station, and checks over her daypack, methodically, several times. Three liters of water, lunch, energy bar, map, hat, sunblock, warm clothes in case God forbid anything should happen and she gets stuck out there longer than usual. Her only luxury item is a notepad to jot down ideas.

Weeks ago, she'd decided that her hike would be along a long wadi about twenty kilometers north of Eilat. Nothing too challenging, but a long, good, and quiet walk, nearly from the western border of the country to the east, all across empty desert, with plenty of time to listen to the way the wind swirls in the wilderness. So Yonit waits not for the express back to Jerusalem, but for a second local bus to the northwest, anticipating the bright, open day ahead; elated that she has succeeded so far; partially amazed that her plan appears to be working; and feeling, in a sense, that the future has become for her altogether brighter, with little motes of freedom reflecting the sunlight amid the dust. The air is already warm, but Yonit is prepared for this too, of

shacharit – morning prayers
ahavat hashem – love of God

course. She is first in line for the bus, and as she boards, she tells the driver where she wants to get off. He nods.

One might imagine a different driver questioning this sixteen-year-old girl about her intentions to hike alone in the desert, even refusing to let her off unaccompanied. But this driver, though only thirty-one, has seen all kinds of people do all kinds of things, and it isn't his job to advise them otherwise. He has his own life to worry about, and doesn't much care about this posh Ashkenazi girl, setting out on her little hike while his wife and two children still lie asleep in their small home at the northern edge of Eilat. Though Yonit feels in this moment that she is writing her own story at last, in fact, the driver is one of many co-authors of a narrative whose roots and branches spread out in many directions. A half hour later, he calls out the stop Yonit has requested. It comes sooner than she expected; there is no cell service in this remote part of the desert, and Yonit is the only one getting off; she has to take a moment to fold up her map. The soldiers look at her. Her face flushes with embarrassment. She rushes off the bus, which pulls away in a cloud of noise. Yonit looks around for the trailhead and finds it. And then, gradually, as her heart stops pounding—silence.

I want to suggest that, but for a chance accident three hours into the hike, all might have gone very well for Yonit. There is a sense in which we might read her story backward, from where Yonit finds herself at the end to the various decisions that brought her to that point. But this would be, I propose, a misreading. Even after the accident, which I will shortly describe, things could still have gone differently for her. There is no such thing as fate, really; our choices are merely our choices, small contributions overshadowed by randomness and luck. We are not the sole authors of our stories, and often what seem like the consequences of our actions are, in fact, mere intrusions of luck. Yonit imagines the guiding hand of God shaping her life and informing it, and perhaps she will still hold this belief in the end. Perhaps you hold such beliefs as well. And perhaps this sort of God does exist, though there would be a great deal to account for if so. Yet even if there exists some causal machinery that we do not understand, it is so inscrutable as to be impossible to render in a narrative. I would not want to propose that Yonit was *destined* to fall off a boulder—not even a large boulder, really more of a large rock, just a few feet tall—or that this accident was determined by her choices; or was a kind of recompense for them; or that it was fate, determined from the beginning. Of course, you are free to interpret the tale in this way, but that choice lies with you. To be sure, if I simply told you about the hike, and the fall, and the freak occurrence of Yonit's full plastic water bottle breaking on the fall, you would be justified in thinking that I believe, in this tale at least, that all reflects some Divine will, or perhaps an ordered operation of the universe: reap, sow, give, receive. It would be reasonable to infer that I believe such things do not just happen, in stories or in life. Everything may be interpreted. Yet I do not believe this. Everything may be left uninterpreted as well; God is a choice of the exegete. Possibly Yonit's accident has, in itself, no meaning at all; our choices are based on our desires and dreams, but what ultimately comes of them is as much chance as intention. And if this latter non-interpretation engenders a kind of anomie, the former is frequently obscene.

The facts, then, only. It is three hours into the hike, which has been pleasant and delightfully uneventful, although not entirely as contemplative as Yonit had hoped, if only because she is so excited about it. Her mind has been racing, darting from plan to thought to idea. Stop thinking like the organized girl who has everything planned out, she tells herself, enjoy the experience more in the moment. This is not an itinerary: this is the trip itself. This is what you had planned for—this is the wide, open place—stop constantly thinking about this in terms of your plans and your success and you and your noise—*shhhh*—don't think of each plant like Rachel does, as something put there by design and part of her world of God and mitzvot and responsibility, because that's what you are doing when you think its importance is to *you*, and the experience that *you* wanted to have—stop thinking and let the place be the place. So Yonit makes a special effort to slow down, relax, and listen to the ambient sounds of the desert. From her map, she can tell that she is making better time than expected; she is walking quickly and taking few breaks. She has finished almost all of her first bottle of water, which is a bit ahead of schedule, so she has slowed down her drinking to better ration the remainder. And so she can afford to slow down her pace as well. At one point, she sees a small herd of hyraxes, little badger-like creatures that hop among the rocks, and regrets that she is unable to take any photographs, since they might later become evidence of her transgression.

It is shortly after this encounter that the accident to which I have referred takes place. As part of her deliberate slowing down, Yonit decides to stray a bit from the path to get a view of a particular byway of the wadi. She walks for a couple of minutes with no trail in front of her, but soon becomes tired of clambering over the rocks and among the delicate plants she is afraid of crushing underfoot. And it has gotten very hot. So Yonit climbs up a small boulder to get a look at this odd little side-canyon of the wadi, intending to turn back after taking in the view. She stands in the sun, unshaded for a few moments at the mouth of the narrow inlet, and realizes she has grown dizzy. She reaches into her backpack to take a drink of water, and she knows it—she knows it before it happens, at the moment her balance is shifted improperly, maybe it was the lack of water that caused her balance to be off, or maybe just bad luck—she can feel herself beginning to fall. And, in that moment before she does fall, she begins to hope and to calculate the odds and to think about how to minimize any damage. Her instinct is to protect her head, of course, and she picks up her arms reflexively, which seems to make her lose her balance even more, and Yonit falls off of the boulder, letting out only a tiny, barely audible cry as she does.

The backpack breaks her fall, which Yonit immediately thinks is good luck, despite the pain already shooting up her legs and arms. It could have been her head. God is watching out for her after all, even here in these narrow places. Yonit utters a quick prayer of thanksgiving and then inspects the damage: she is scraped up, but nothing serious. It will be okay, she thinks, just—far. Yonit realizes that she is scared, her heart pounding and her body flushed with adrenaline. What is she *doing* out here? Who does she think she is, hiking alone in the desert? Who does such a stupid thing? There is a difference between taking a vacation and being a fool.

It is only as Yonit stands up, hesitantly, that she realizes her backpack is soaking wet. For a brief, pre-rational moment, she fears it is blood. She is hurt! But then, she realizes this cannot be—so what is it? She takes off the pack, and sees what has happened. Somehow the second water bottle—the full one—has cracked, split. Against the rocks, no doubt. It is made of heavy plastic, but it was a hard fall, and Yonit landed squarely on it. The water! Yonit hurriedly takes out the empty bottle, and tries to rescue as much as she can from the broken one. But she manages to save only a cupful, at most. The rest is already soaked into the material of the pack, and into the sweatshirt that she brought in case of emergency.

Quickly Yonit extracts the map, still mostly dry, from the front pocket of the backpack. Her phone seems to be working, although there is still no service here in the wilderness. The thing to do now is get out. The vacation part is over. But, Yonit realizes, she has almost no water, and is in virtually the dead center of the walk. What's more, she has descended with the wadi these last few hours, to the point that to retrace her steps, which might be a bit wiser in terms of knowing the terrain she is to face, would be much harder going: all uphill, all of it. The way the hike was planned, there was meant to be more descent than ascent. So the best way to proceed is probably to go on. But, with her aching legs, it might take hours, and who knows what lies ahead. And she has begun to feel faint. So much for rationing the water, Yonit thinks, I need more water, soon. When am I likely to meet someone? I am shaken up, that's all; but not all, because I am injured, a little, and because I am thirsty, very thirsty, and now tired, and dizzy, from the heat. The heat which now seems unrelenting.

Yonit decides to press forward. She admits to herself that part of the reason may be that she still *wants* to go forward, to not let it all go to waste, after all this planning and all this success, but really, the logic is there—not only is the walk ahead likely to be easier than the walk back (one can't be sure, but there are probabilities), but in under an hour the path crosses the Israel Trail, which is likely to have other hikers on it, people from whom Yonit could beg a little water and maybe some help.

The walk is hard going. Yonit is stretching the last cup of water as best she can, but it is already half gone within half an hour; one can only drink so little at a time. And where is the intersection with the trail? Back in Jerusalem, Yonit had chosen her route according to what she thought would be the least-traveled path; solitude is what she had wanted. But now, she desperately wishes to encounter someone, anyone with just a little water, and maybe some help, or a way to communicate with the outside world, like the soldiers have, radios that work where there is no phone service. She begins to feel dizzier. I cannot pass out, Yonit thinks, not here in the desert. I have to stay awake. The wet pack mocks her as it presses up against her back, making her uncomfortably damp even as she hopes that, somehow, her body is absorbing some of the water. The bruises have begun to form, and the pain adds to the dizziness.

Finally, Yonit reaches the Israel Trail, after almost ninety minutes. She waits at the crossroads for almost a full hour more, reciting tehillim in order to stay awake, asking God if this was the test that she had unwittingly asked for, and apologizing for only believing in God now in her moment of need. Yonit is certain that someone will soon be coming up or down the trail—but no one does. Impossible! True, it is a weekday, and approaching the heat of the day, and in summer, but still—no one for an hour? She ponders turning onto the trail on the theory that there will be more people on it, but it doesn't lead in the right direction; if she fails to encounter anyone, it would be hours before she would reach a road or town of any kind. No: better to move forward, in the direction of the eastern road. Someone, eventually, will have to turn up. Yonit wonders at the crossroads if she should yell for help, but thinks better of it. Really, would anyone hear? It's amazing that no one has come along! But it is only two more hours of walking until the road; people go three times as long with nothing to drink, Yonit thinks, and I've already had almost two liters today. It's not like that has disappeared from history. It is in me. I'll be fine. I just wish I weren't so . . . dizzy. But it is hot—very hot. I would take off my shirt if I wouldn't burn underneath. I don't care about being embarrassed, or modest. I wish I could be like those boys who, when they are hot, simply take off more and more clothes, she thinks, her thoughts rambling. Yonit remembers one time hiking with her school in the Ramon Crater, on a day almost as hot as this one, and how all the boys complained about the heat even though they had nothing left on their bodies but shorts and sandals. Whereas Yonit and her friends were still wearing heavy shirts, bras, and skirts, at once admiring the boys' bodies and resenting them. To be as free as they are, so free they no longer remember to be grateful!

Finally Yonit decides to walk onward. There is no point in sitting still, not getting anywhere. Now it has been more than five hours since the start of the hike, nearly two hours since she has had anything to drink, and, looking at the map, likely two more hours, at this slow pace, until she will reach the road to the east. The distances seem longer than expected. Yonit curses the plastic bottle that broke so easily on the fall. Plastic isn't supposed to break like that! she repeats, almost aloud. I planned properly! Yonit's legs have grown tired and her head is spinning. She needs a rest, a short rest, and then she can continue. Just a short rest. After all, the Bedouins, Yonit had read, sleep in the heat of the day, and wake to continue on in the late afternoon. I will do the same, she thinks.

Yonit looks around. Although there are no caves or real shelter visible nearby, there are acacia trees everywhere in this part of the desert, their branches twisting and dividing outward. They invite her, it seems, to sit underneath them. They beckon, like the *kikayon* of Yonit's namesake, Jonah: come here, and rest, and be happy underneath me. Yonit ponders this voice that seems to be speaking to her in the quiet desert. They speak as if tempting her to make the wrong decision, to let down her guard when she should not—to indulge, to risk. Yonit has read all about these acacia trees, the atzei shittim, at once worshipped by the other nations in Canaan, millennia ago (*avodah zara*, she hears Rachel's voice say in her head) and also the sacred wood of the *ohel moed*, the *mishkan* itself! Out of these same trees the Israelites constructed the holy mishkan, which they dedicated to Hashem. These trees, if they are pagan trees, are also our trees, our holy trees; they are the trees with which we devote ourselves to God. And, it was said, the acacia bark was used in the sacred incense in the *beit hamikdash*, inducing visions, prophecies. Hashem! It is You after all! Speaking through the trees, Your sacred Shechinah! It is only avodah zara to separate the tree from God. This is not temptation, but God *nistar*, concealed in the tree, until You are revealed. The Canaanites with their avodah zara and their *k'deshim*— that is their only mistake! The cleaving and the separation, the breaking of the vessel and the forgetting of its origin.

Yonit finds the largest acacia she can see and sits at its base. She mops her forehead with her wet sweatshirt, hoping

kikayon – mythical plant that sheltered the prophet Jonah
avodah zara – idolatry
ohel moed – the biblical "tent of meeting"
mishkan – the biblical Tabernacle
beit hamikdash – the Temple

to squeeze another drop of water from it into her mouth. It is hot. In the shade of the tree, Yonit finally does take off her shirt and her bra, since there is no one around and she is so uncomfortable. No more modesty now; now, comfort. It is my turn, Yonit thinks, and my right. Anyway, even if someone did come by, they would make noise first, and so what? This is a matter of life and death! Yonit imagines that the voice of God in the tree, its crackling sound like an insect whenever the wind blows, is calling out to her in the same way the freedom of the woman on the bus called out to her and in the same way she wants to call to the scholar boy who sits quietly in the corner, hiding his dreams. The breeze feels delicious on her breasts. She is delighted by the notion of her friends seeing her now and being shocked. She feels at home at last, with the quiet, not among all that meaningless *mepatpet*, the chatter of silly schoolgirls, but under the rustling of these branches. At last I am home, with Hashem, alone. If only I had water, she thinks, this would be Gan Eden. This is freedom: this vast, quiet space, dotted with trees like this one, offering shelter. The sun beats down, but the tree protects.

Yonit sits upright under the tree, takes off her hiking boots and her socks. Her tired bare feet feel the deliciousness of rest and air. She is grateful to the tree, giving her shade, allowing her to rest amid its branches, whispering to her. She can understand why ancients could worship the trees that bring such relief from the unrelenting sun. The breeze that rustles its branches caresses her chest. She hugs the tree, kisses its sacred bark with its unknown magic, imagines she can taste it. And then something happens: the light shining through the branches becomes prismatic, fractal, rotating in patterns and color. I am passing out, Yonit thinks, but she remains awake, only also asleep, again like her namesake Jonah, in his trance on the boat with the sailors. Yonit sees the scholar boy like before, only this time he is naked, and stepping toward her. "Holy," he whispers. And now she too is naked, feeling his body tickle against hers. She reaches to touch him, and touches his face, unshaven but smooth, and she looks in his eyes. He is still wearing his kippah. Yonit now sees the Canaanites and their idols: masks, statues, gods with huge phalluses and goddesses with enormous breasts, and their rituals, too, of *yichud* in their holy of holies. She feels fire. The fire grows hotter, and she is thirsty. Those gods are watching the scholar boy enter her, but he is not her master: she surrounds him, his face distorted by lust, his chest tensed and flexed, she controls him. And when Yonit looks into the boy's face she sees for a moment David Pereg, grimacing as he drives into her, but presently his face is replaced by that of Shlomit Hazony, the girl they called a whore; but Shlomit is on top of her, and Yonit is the scholar boy underneath, and now it is the spirit of the tree pushing into her, in the desert, under the hot sun.

But then Yonit hears a voice. "Yonit," it calls out, "have you lost your way?" It is Yonit's Aunt Chana, the one who died, calling to her from within the acacia tree. Yonit moves to speak, but cannot, and so replies in her mind only: "Chana." *Cheyn*, she hears to herself, descendant of hesed, sister of netzach; and Yonit sees Chana before her, Chana, whose life was so hard and cut short in such a way by the rage of judgment unleashed; Chana, intertwined with the branches of the acacia tree. Had Chana not merited an ascent to shamayim? Was she trapped here in the tree? Or was she—was she waiting for this moment? And is she here to return me to the world of the living, or to take me with her, with a kiss, as it is written? Yonit looks into Chana's eyes but cannot make out an answer. Part of Yonit wants this consummation, to finally leave behind the world that she has known, to join Chana and Hashem in silence. But Yonit also thinks of her parents, her sisters, her friends, and wants to go back to them, to spare them this heartache, to continue. She feels Chana's presence calling her back. And so she opens her eyes. Suddenly, beyond the branches, unsure whether it is real or a dream, but in front of the brambles, Yonit thinks she sees, for a moment, the scholar boy again: a curious, puzzled face looking down at her.

This scholar boy is real; his name is Yaniv; he lives in Eilat and hikes in the desert often. Like Yonit, Yaniv is sixteen years old; he comes from a "traditional" family, but his religiosity is different from Yonit's, and more at home with magic. His friends are eating lunch not far away; he decided to explore this byway on his own. It is not unusual for him to be here: for Yaniv and his friends, the desert is their park. But never has he seen anything like this: a beautiful, pale girl, half-naked, half-dazed, lying alone in the middle of the desert! It seems to him like a pornographic video one might watch on a boring school night. What is she doing here? Now Yaniv, too, faces a choice, but not really a choice, as morally there is no question: he has to help her. But Yaniv also hears another voice: *Do it.* He wants her, desires her, now. No one will know, no one is watching but the trees, and the trees don't care. Yaniv feels lust rising inside of him. Maybe she won't even remember, she seems delirious. Maybe no one will ever know.

But then the girl opens her eyes. Yaniv sees that she sees him, and freezes. He feels relieved, as if he'd been led to a precipice but now, thankfully, has been brought back. But Yonit is only a hair's breadth on the side of life, and from that vantage point, she hears many voices: the tree goddess whispering, *take him, devour him, envelop him in my branches*; Aunt Chana's voice whispering Yonit's name, whether drawing her onward or backward. Which of these is the voice of Hashem, Yonit wonders, in whom I trust and do not fear? Or are there many voices after all? All this Yonit considers in an instant.

If Yonit hesitates much longer, she and Yaniv will remember themselves; the suspension of time will cease, identity will return, and the conditions of their upbringing will resume their influence. They have their lives, their families, their schools where only one side of the story is taught. And who is to say? Perhaps that partiality is for the best, given human nature and the evil inclination, as Aunt Chana herself came to know. Maybe the angels of virtue are right and the gods of lust are wrong; maybe there really are good kids and bad kids, and the bad ones eventually are lost in the wilderness.

But for a brief moment, there is a nexus of potentiality, of branches spreading out from the tree trunk, of the coursing and dividing of the rivers flowing from Eden, and in that instant, there is infinite potentiality. Is it possible to know the way the water will run and the branches will grow? Maybe there is no end to what we would need to know: the slippery rock, the death of Aunt Chana, the way Yonit talked to David Pereg; uncounted causes and conditions. But even if we were to know them, is it not the meaning of freedom that we cannot know which of the gods will be victorious in this moment, and whether it is possible to cross the space between them?

THE TRANSFIGURATION

The band launched into a slow-building dirge, built on klezmer foundations but repeating, evolving, raga-like, on the structure of a few simple lines, themselves excerpted from a classic *niggun*: minor key, sadness and joy intermingled, the texture somehow shiny and worn at the same time. Dana and Yoram set the tempo—gradual, almost shuffling, lilting. Raphael, on clarinet, introduced the main theme, which Gabriel played with him on trumpet, their two instruments melding into two sides of a harmonic whole. The melody contorted itself gently, slunk up sideways, with the traditional minor notes accentuating the graceful twist of the tune. Sitting in, a guitarist from the old downtown scene, Arlo Tremaine, fell in tentatively with a recurring pulse in the root note, which brought out each cadence of the drums. Chai Rubin sat in on piano, accenting the evolution of the theme with a few, spare chords.

It was vintage Pintele Yid, the band Gabriel and Raphael had founded nearly a decade ago now. Everything was fair game, from lilting Hasidic melodies to Sun Ra space jazz, Soft Machine–like prog grooves to Eastern European

niggun – wordless Hasidic melody

stomps. The freedom was exuberant: Gabriel's horn would cry with the sighs of the shtetl one moment, soar like Miles over Gil Evans the next. Pintele Yid had its roots in New York's queer klezmer scene; their audiences were small but appreciative, earnest but not naïve, part of the progressive Brooklyn bubble in all the best ways. But their fans stretched beyond that world as well. The band played small festivals and clubs; held unpublicized Wednesday-night jam sessions at out-of-the-way spots in Gowanus, East New York, and Bed-Stuy; and had earned the respect of New York's alternative jazz scene, well beyond Jewish circles. Raphael was the one who kept it all together—a kind of neo-hippie clarinetist/keyboardist/occasional percussionist who wore big knitted yarmulkes and went on spiritual retreats. His charisma was inescapable, he was the showman, the yang to Gabriel's yin. Dana Katz was alternately a cool breeze and a tornado on drums, her sticks flying with syncopated rhythms; and Yoram Oz on bass was laconic until the spotlight shone on him, and suddenly: there was revelation.

Chai took the first solo, their fingers somehow dancing and pausing at the same time, throwing bits of Monk and Hancock into the old-world setting. The sudden blue notes had a dissonant feel, which Chai felt right away, and then, seemingly out of chutzpah, they turned them into crashing chords that seemed to embody the collision of cultures. The rhythm section lunged forward, now at the pace of a wheel on a horse-drawn carriage. They edged the tempo upward; Chai responded with swirls of notes that seemed at once Hasidic and bebop and both. Gabriel felt a little high, the

THC he'd eaten earlier breaking the blood-brain barrier, helping him to listen intently to the conversation unfolding around him as if dropping into a mikva. Normally he would take the next solo, but Raphael motioned that he wanted to go—and he was the front man. So in Raphael went, rocking his body back and forth with every note, the rhythm a dervish now, spinning, passing each familiar melodic phrase with increasing frequency, like the waving of your mother's hand when you hurl by her on a merry-go-round when you're five or six years old. The crowd erupted in the middle of the solo, couldn't help themselves, as Raphael cascaded the phrases around each other, careening into a high wail that, somehow, the rest of the band knew was coming, and they all paused for a moment at the top of the roller coaster, taking in the view, knowing what was next, expecting it, and then rushed headlong into a furious storm of joy and sadness and minor sevenths.

It was paradise, it was a burst of life, of eros, of everything that, for Gabriel, made life worth living. It was the essence of everything he considered holy.

* * *

But all this had come at a cost. Years ago, Gabriel committed his life to music. *Seize the day*, he had told himself when he was younger. *Stay true to yourself, don't give up.* All of the words that young people promise to themselves. And yet, while Gabriel was successful as a musician, he wasn't a superstar, even in klezmer terms, and almost no one in that world could sustain themselves financially through music anyway. Everyone who hadn't inherited or married into real money had a side hustle, usually more than one: session work and teaching students, sure, but also driving cars, fixing toilets, cleaning, painting—anything, really. And of course, endless *simchas*. There was a romance to it, suffering for art and all that, but also an endless uphill climb, constant anxiety, and no health insurance.

Many times, Gabriel had considered putting down his horn and doing something more sustainable—something that would let him buy instead of rent, or get out from under the mountain of student-loan debt that would surely accompany him to his grave. But Gabriel had just turned forty; even before Pintele Yid, he'd been doing this a long time. What had once been a calling had become, it seemed, a rather unprofitable career. Onstage, or in jam sessions, the magic still happened more often than not: sparks of incandescent joy, tears of broken melodies, inexpressibly poignant phrases that evoked the suffering of the Jewish people and the yearning for transcendence. But then there was the rest of the time.

Moreover, Gabriel increasingly felt as though he was living at some remove from his own experience, especially his own body. As passionate as he was onstage, his love life offstage was arid; he'd been in only three long-term relationships in the last fifteen years, and felt emotionally ill at ease, as if he were playing a role in someone else's life. There were always

simcha – joy, happy occasion

plenty of opportunities for sex of all kinds—though Gabriel was primarily straight, everyone in the scene around the band seemed to be in a kind of rhapsodic, joyous exploration of all permutations of queerness, kink, poly this and nonbinary that. And while he had experimented sexually with all varieties of people, still there seemed a kind of remove, a distance, as if lust was happening to someone else, as if Gabriel were witnessing desire rather than truly immersing in it. For a while, Gabriel hoped that by exploring queer desire, he might find the source of his dissociation from both lust and love: maybe he was actually gay, still working through internalized homophobia; maybe if he met the right person, he would feel what others seemed to feel all around him: not even necessarily romantic love, but even lust that felt like more than the mere secretion of dopamine. But queerness didn't seem to be the answer. There was a thrill, at first, in overcoming his own fear and resistance, and for a time Gabriel mistook that thrill to be desire. But that faded with familiarity; the permutations of anatomy and gender were no longer taboo, or even liberating. And so, increasingly, he felt like an interloper in the entire queer scene—as if he were queer in name only, not queer enough, not deserving of the label at all. It wasn't lost on Gabriel that the desire in his music existed in tension with the desirelessness of his body. But the yearning in Gabriel's music was more a yearning to yearn. It was as Rebbe Nachman of Breslov once taught: if one cannot speak to God, one yearns to speak; and if one cannot yearn, one yearns to yearn.

"When a person is out of balance," Rav Moishe Lander

had told Gabriel at their weekly *shiur*, "the world for that person is out of balance. Even prophecy is heard by the prophet in his own voice. God's voice is not other than your own. And when your own *middos*, the qualities of your own personality, are out of order, this disorder is the voice of God that you hear."

"How does a person change that?" Gabriel asked.

"The miracle of the *hesed* from above is that it flows even when it blocked," Rabbi Lander replied. "There is always the possibility to open the channels. This is the difference between the way of Torah and the way of modern man: we both see the same universe, but those who believe know that there is an extra small amount of love—an extra bit of hesed. It comes to us in moments of *hod*, of splendor, of grace, when we glimpse something beyond the material world. Perhaps you experience this in your music. Yet sometimes, the Kabbalah teaches us that this extra hesed is also the source of evil, because it is in a state of superfluity, as it were, to all that is. It is out of balance. Perhaps one is not meant to receive this aspect of the shefa, perhaps one's true place is otherwise. It is knowing where one stands, Gavriel"—the rabbi paused and looked Gabriel in the eye—"that is the difference between those who believe, and those who don't."

Gabriel was not a believer. Not once did he imagine that God was listening, or had ever listened, or could ever be said to listen, to the words of human beings; Gabriel had

shiur – lesson

always been adjacent to faith. Yet still he drank deep from its wells, not only of klezmer songs, wordless niggunim, and the inflections of the *mama loshen*, but also of the mystical piety of the old Hasidim; the life infused with ritual and prayer, which he occasionally sampled in old, decrepit shuls in Brooklyn and on the Lower East Side; and above all, the wailing, the yearning, the ever-present awareness, it seemed to Gabriel, of the dark. His shiurim with Rav Moishe, held one-on-one in a cluttered study in the Landers' apartment in Crown Heights, were part of this passion, and part of what gave Gabriel solace during difficult times. It wasn't that Gabriel believed in Rav Moishe's mysticism as a matter of faith, and he always resisted his attempts to bring him into deeper Jewish observance. But he could feel the desperation to *have* faith, the same plaintive cry that his trumpet let slip as it wound its tones around an old Hasidic niggun. The act of wailing was itself significant—the most exasperated, desperate act of the human soul; the pure expression of essential human desire. His trumpet's cries came from this place; his love of the wailing Jews did as well. That, he had long held, was true religion.

* * *

Now it was Arlo's turn to solo, and so he did, slicing and shredding the melody into fragments of half-phrases and dissonant chords. It was like klezmer dissected and reas-

mama loshen – Yiddish (lit. "mother tongue")

sembled into some kind of avant-jazz monster; it was hard and beautiful and shiny like the rough rocks and sand that scrape your toes at the beach. Gabriel nodded along, adding a couple of accent notes here and there, biding his time.

And there, in the wings, was the kid.

He had just shown up one night at a club in Gowanus—somehow he'd heard about one of the jam sessions, had brought his trumpet, wanted to play. Dovid, he said was his name, though despite the Yiddish pronunciation he wasn't wearing a kippah. Couldn't have been more than fifteen, sixteen, Gabriel thought, still had a somehow effeminate way of walking, like he was still just hitting puberty. He asked if he could play—and why not, it was a jam session, not a gig, it was open to all comers—for a few bars anyway. "Sure, kid," Raphael said. "Try to follow along." And that's what the kid did, obeying dutifully, falling in with the band on a standard niggun that everyone knew by heart. He was good enough, he knew how to play and keep up—not bad, really. Raphael glanced over at Gabriel, they both raised their eyebrows, and nodded toward the kid: the next solo would be his.

And then it happened. The kid started with a few sturdy notes, each held for a while longer or shorter than expected—safe territory, good idea, thought Gabriel—just bringing us in, but then, out of nowhere—it was like when you're running or biking or sailing in a strong wind, and you have your direction and your intention, but then the wind comes up and gusts suddenly, and blows you at an angle you'd never run at before—like that, out from nowhere, came a whole new reading of the melody, at twice the speed, four times the speed, but never rushed, like a different language being spoken in the room with its intonations and emphases and a vocabulary all its own, which you never knew before but which, now, you'd never forget. And behind it, the kid's technique was perfect—where had he learned?—and his respect for the tradition was evident; this wasn't only flash, it was also *knowledge*, the intimate kind, the kind that comes from instinct, but meets erudition, and gives birth to something new. Gabriel heard him quote at least two niggunim that he'd heard only once before, from an old *hazzan* he learned with a few years back. And yet there was also something original—some kind of creation taking place. Raphael waved him on for another sixteen. It was as if the kid had discovered a new formula, the fourth chord, the missing link. You looked at him, with his angel-smooth face and Converse sneakers, and you wondered whether he'd started playing horn in the womb.

Eventually the solo wound its way back to its beginning, and the band came in. There were only a few people there, beside the players, but they broke into river-rushing applause. Something had happened.

Gabriel's solo was anticlimax. Had to be. No matter what he would do, it wouldn't be as present, as *this is actually happening*, as what had just taken place. Gabriel suggested the answers he had composed to Raphael's previous solo, but now they seemed to be part of an obsolete dialogue, dated

hazzan – cantor

and meaningless. It was as though the two of them were arguing a point of theology when they had just witnessed revelation.

After the jam session, everyone gathered around the kid. "Where'd you learn to play like that, kid?" Raphael asked, wiping sweat off his brow.

"I've taken some lessons, I guess," Dovid replied, blushing.

"With who?" It was no one they had heard of.

"He's kind of old and all?" Dovid said, suddenly a kid again, speaking with the inflections of a teenager. "And, he used to play, but not anymore? So, yeah."

"Well he's done a great job," said Gabriel. The kid blushed some more.

"Dovid, I hope you can come out next Wednesday night when we're playing again. We'd love to have you sit in," said Raphael. "Maybe we can get more time to talk."

"Sure," Dovid said. And so he did. He came to the next jam session, and Raphael invited him to a gig, and he played along, and people talked about it, so he sat in on the next gig too. Of course Gabriel felt a pang of envy, but the world was big enough for two trumpet players, right? He had even found himself trying to recreate snatches of the melodies that the kid had seemed to play off the cuff. It wasn't easy— they weren't quoting from anything Gabriel had heard before, and he couldn't quite master it. The notes seemed to have come from somewhere else entirely.

Meanwhile, the kid's reputation was growing. People who hadn't come through for Pintele Yid in years came to see the kid. And Gabriel noticed that the kid had picked up some affectations: now he wore a cap on his mop of unwashed brown hair, his tight clothes seemed a little more deliberately composed . . . the kid was doing a look! But the playing was for real. For a time, it made Gabriel's own work better, having this second trumpet in the band, like a disciple or an apprentice, although, of course, also a genius. Everything about the kid was beautiful; he lived up to his namesake. But gradually, seemingly inevitably, Gabriel's shared joy became interlaced with jealousy and resentment. The kid was growing more famous than the rest of the band, and everyone knows you can't have two trumpet players in a klezmer five-piece. So what would that mean for Gabriel? It seemed fundamentally unfair. Compared with Gabriel's years of work, what had the kid sacrificed, what dues had he paid? None, it seemed. And now Raphael was telling Gabriel that a couple of record people were coming to the gig at Marian's, which was great, you know, a *commercial* opportunity, as Raphael had said over the phone. The logic was inescapable: just some better gigs would make a difference, let alone a real record deal. But logic is always escapable.

"Do you know the story of Rabbi Elimelech and the shepherd boy?" Rav Moishe asked, when Gabriel told him about the kid.

"It sounds familiar, but . . ."

"Once, Rabbi Elimelech was sitting on the bimah on Yom Kippur. The yiddin are praying, but Rav Elimelech ascends to heaven and finds their prayers are not being accepted. He prays harder, with all the secret *kavvanos* that he knows, that he learned from his teacher, to somehow merit acceptance and sweeten the dinim with hesed from the kadosh boruch hu, but nothing seems to be working.

"Meanwhile there is a shepherd boy, an ignoramus, who has only heard that this is an important day on which the sins of Israel are forgiven. He goes to the shul, where he's never been before, but of course he doesn't know how to pray, or even read. All he knows is how to play a simple shepherd's flute, which he carries around with him. So he takes out his flute and starts to play.

"Of course, several of the members of the congregation quickly turn to shush him. Playing a flute in shul on Yom Kippur! But Rabbi Elimelech sees that the shepherd's melody is a prayer, and because of his abilities as a tzaddik he can see that this prayer is accepted by God where the others were not. Because the shepherd boy's song is offered with his full heart, from the depths of his *neshama*. And so Rabbi Elimelech tells the congregation not to interfere. And it is by the merit of the shepherd boy's prayer, played on his flute, that the community is spared."

Perhaps these words were meant to be a comfort, but as he heard them, Gabriel felt pain—rage, even, that the efforts of the congregation meant nothing in comparison with the unlearned ease of a shepherd boy, that a life spent dedicated to something, devoted to a craft, was so meaningless in the eyes of the Holy One. And so unjust! Some of us are simply

kavvanos – Kabbalistic meanings of prayer

born with this . . . grace? And some are not? Some taste love, others do not; some have a gift, others do not. And who is this cosmic puppet master deciding who by fire and who by drowning? This is who Rav Moishe worships and venerates with every fiber of his being?

"I can't accept that this is just a matter of divine decree, that some are simply gifted with genius, while all the Hasidim—what about them? Had they not suffered too? Was not one among their prayers worthy of being accepted?"

"Gavriel," replied Rav Moishe. "There are many kinds of *kedusha*. All of us are meant to give and to receive according to our middos. When we only try to give, or we give in the wrong place at the wrong time, one may travel down the wrong path."

* * *

So now, Arlo was finished, and out of respect for Gabriel, it had been agreed that Dovid would solo before him. A hush fell over the room as the kid walked out, needing no introduction, nodding at the band and the audience as he took his place onstage; there was a moment of heightened attention: a silence within the sound. And, sure enough, the kid delivered. He picked his way through the melody, not like Arlo tearing it to pieces but like a young child skipping around puddles on a wet sidewalk, nimbly dancing around each note; then in another moment it was like seduction, or even foreplay, teasing the audience and the band with what everyone knew was about to come forth, but making them wait for it, anticipate it, want it. And when it began to burst forth, there was again that sense of music coming from somewhere else. Part of it was the focused attention of the crowd, the hype, the charisma that the kid seemed to have, despite his (practiced?) insouciance, the way the spotlight seemed to create an aura around him. But part of it was that, as before, the kid seemed to be speaking a different language. Who ever thought of *that?* Wait—where's *this* coming from? It was as if he had not only an encyclopedia of references in his head, to quote and twist and recontextualize, but on top of it all the genius, sui generis, coming from nowhere that anyone else had ever been, an ability to translate and transmute every phrase he played until they seemed, after their transformation, to hint at realms unexplored. The kid was beautiful. He was a natural.

And then something happened: after the earthquake and the fire, Gabriel heard in Dovid's playing a delicate, quivering voice say two words only: *let go.*

And with these words, Gabriel Frutiger experienced his own death. He was still alive—indeed, somehow more alive, still standing on the side of the stage at Marian's. But the spotlight, though still on the kid, seemed to surround him; he released into the music in a way he never had before, letting it suffuse him, envelop him, surround and fill him. It was Dovid, of course, but Dovid as a pipe for the Divine flow, the shefa raining down from the supernal realms, but at the same time entirely here, immanent and immediate: the sound, in this room, heard by these people, this breath, these patterns arraying themselves like the sparkling *heikhalot* in the blinding fog of the stage lights; and Gabriel at last entered his body, bathed in music, seeing the sounds at last, somehow able, by grace, to set down a weight he had been carrying for twenty years: there dropped, for a moment, the yearning for more; this was enough, Gabriel knew; this was it. And as Gabriel let Dovid's music inside of him, he wept, because it had unlocked him, revealed what had always been true, but had somehow been kept from him, beyond a hidden portal; he wished to receive and surround and make a womb for this sound, while also resting in the womb of the sound; there was no dichotomy of male and female anymore; there was womb and seed intermingled; there was a transfiguration into multiples, Gavriel, Gevurat-el, Gevira, Gevurat-Ela, Gavriel-Ela: the female-male neitherness of the Goddess, entering and entered, compassionate and boundaried; the *kruvim* in intercourse above the ark, a multiplicity multiplying, each already complete without dichotomy, two seas intertwining without division, an interpenetration of winter-summer moon and earth-ocean heart.

And as if by the river Chebar the spirit entered into Gavriel-Ela, as it is written, and Gavriel beheld the world without their music, the wells of production and insemination at last run dry; and yet there was no barrenness; the world went on exactly as before, perhaps with one sonata less but neither more nor less filled with pain or solace or rapture; it doesn't actually *matter*, Gavriel-Ela felt; I am enough without

heikhalot – heavenly palaces
kruvim – cherubs

these tones; there is no mark one needs to make; this is a man's myth, not mine, wrapped in someone else's sublimated progeniture; it was never mine; it is over. There is already river in the sky and fire in the earth; there is already all that needs to be done.

And with this Gavriel-Ela saw the sound of their own soul quieted, no longer grasping and incomplete, no longer yearning for some exterior consummation; the candle was extinguished and yet everything was brighter than before—Dovid's music; the light; the body, which felt earthy and enflamed, and also like a chrysalis ready to be emerged from; Gavriel-Ela felt the weight of this flesh as they never had before, felt its lacks and superfluities, knew that they were both ocean and vessel, and at once the voice fell silent and there was no need for secrets lying beneath or above; this was enough; Gavriel-Ela was enough; because the burden was set down, done is what needed to be done, and here were these sounds and people and lights, and Gavriel-Ela, the pillar of Asherah, stone-tree sky mother, deep chasm earth-father, receiving Dovid's radiant and glowing light as if anointed in oil everywhere in the body; and in this way Gabriel experienced death.

Suddenly, it was time to play. The kid had finished. There was, for a moment, a pause, as Gabriel's voice had fallen silent. But then a different voice spoke, the sound of the *bat kol*, at once line and cycle, right and left, and thus neither and both together, and it replied: *you are a manuscript of a divine letter*. And no one in the band or the audience had before heard the kind of notes that emerged from Gavriel-

Ela's trumpet, which seemed to somehow expand and enclose simultaneously; they were broken and repaired; they needed nothing, and thus were able to open the gate in a new way, which we have only barely merited to hear in our days, but which one day, Gavriel-Ela, you will play for the anointed one.

THE SABBATEAN OF CENTRAL PARK

If I confess these things to you, Rebbe, I worry you will think that I am mamesh fallen into the realm of the klippos, that my yetzer hora has taken control entirely of me. But you know everything already, Rebbe, you hear everything and you see everyone, so already you know what I'm going to say. I beg you, if there is any place in your heart, Rebbe, where you can find rachmanus for me for what I did and who I am, then please can you set me back on a path to Hashem, because that is what I want more than anything. As you said yourself, when you were still on this level, I mean the human world, the gates of tshuva are always open, it is our special gift, the gift of returning to Hashem, and it is what I want more than anything.

I'm only nineteen, Rebbe, so I know there is time to change, maybe, G-d willing, and you can help me, maybe, or maybe, I know Rebbe Nachman recommended saying tehillim for this problem, but . . . I'm not attracted to women. I'm not saying, chas v'sholem, that I'm one of those people who march in the parades as if they are proud of

yetzer hora – evil inclination, specifically the sexual urge

tshuva – repentance

chas v'sholem – God forbid

their perversion. But now with some of the other bochurim at the yeshiva meeting possible shiduchim, it's not . . . it disgusts me, it makes me mamesh physically sick to think of it. It's horrible, I know, because pru urvu is one of the most important mitzvos, and we should always find within us some part of ourselves that loves G-d enough to triumph over the yetzer hora, and it's a z'chus really to have this special burden that Hashem has blessed us with to see if we are worthy. But that is what I have to tell you about, the time I understood the ikker of the problem, this question of the yetzer hora and what it is.

But first I have to admit to you that it isn't only an urge. It's hard to say it out loud to you, Rebbe, but—I've done some things. Just a little, except the time that I'm going to tell you about. Mostly with strangers. Not with any of the other bochurim, chas v'sholem, in fact no one in the yeshiva knows, and I've never talked about it with anyone—not the rebbeim, not my parents, no one. Rebbe, there are these places. Where men go to do things with other men. They are disgusting places. When people talk about the realm of the klippos hatmayos, I know, because I have been there. They call them bathhouses but they're not bathhouses really, like the shvitz or something. They're like mazes, only filled with men who go there to be with other men. One time, only one time, I went into one of the bars they have, the gay

shiduchim – arranged matches

z'chus – merit

ikker – essence

klippos hatmayos – "shells" that are totally impure

bars, in Manhattan. I had taken the train in one Sunday, and I was just wandering around, and I saw the flag that they have, with the rainbow, and I knew that I shouldn't go into this place, but my yetzer had control of me and I took off my hat and put on a baseball cap and went in. The place smelled like liquor, like after a tisch when there's spilled wine everywhere. There were only a few men there, in the afternoon, and they were older men, sitting at the bar watching TV, or standing with their backs against the wall, which had dirty posters on it. One of the men looked at me, like he was surprised to see someone frum there and maybe he knew, I don't know, but I was afraid and so I turned to leave. Then I saw these little magazines by the door, and I took one, and hid it in my jacket, and as soon as I left, I went into an alleyway and read it. Most of the magazine was just a few articles, and advertisements, maybe a few pictures of men with other men at parties or something like that, just pictures. In the back was a section about places you could meet men for sex. It goes to show how one avera can lead to another.

One Motzei Shabbos I went to one of these places. I brought with me the same baseball cap and some secular clothes so no one would know I was Chabad or even Jewish if they weren't looking. You know, I don't really have a beard so it's not obvious, which I think is important because chas v'sholem this would be an insult to You or to Chabad, which

tisch – Hasidic Shabbat celebration
avera – sin
Motzei Shabbos – Saturday night

I could never want. Honestly I could never do it, I don't know if you believe me. This place was—you go in off the street and it seems normal at first. But when you get in, all you can smell is sex and sweat, and you can barely see because it's mamesh almost totally dark. It is a descent into the realm of the klippos. Most of the men were older than me, and they wanted to touch me, or to put their mouths down there, or whatever, and I let them, mostly. I didn't do much to them in return. They didn't seem to care, I guess because I was so young compared to them. I should mention that most of the time you're walking around naked in this place, it's not like you have to go somewhere and take off your clothes. Also I should mention that I tucked my payes back behind my ears so that no one should know. I knew I wouldn't meet anyone who would know what payes are anyway, but I did it to be on the safe side.

So I'm coming to the point, why I'm telling you about the bathhouse. I was getting ready to leave, when I overheard someone talking about how he had just been to the Ramble, which is part of Central Park, and he'd had sex there. He said it like it was no big deal, like everyone knew, which maybe they did. I thought at least that would be better than here, thrown into this pit, like Yosef, with the smells and the sounds of men groaning like animals, where mamesh you could sense the evil, in a place so cut off from every spark of G-d. I want to tell you: I let the men touch me, but we didn't have sex, I mean, actual mishkov zakhar, because for

mishkov zakhar – homosexual acts

two reasons. One, I thought they might have diseases, in fact
I'm sure some of them did. Two, even though I knew that I
was committing a horrible avera even being with these men,
I thought, it would be even worse if I did that, because that
was mamesh right in Vayikra, to lie with a man as you lie
with a woman, and it is a to'evah, so I thought to myself,
look it's bad enough doing what you're doing, but at least it
doesn't have to be the worst.

So, the next day, I went to Central Park, and that is what
I have to tell you about, even though I'd rather talk about
mamesh anything else in the world. I feel like even saying
these words, if you can hear me, is calling up the forces from
the klippos, and I'm hoping that wherever you are you can
protect me from them.

It was just after Pesach, so the weather was warm already
with spring. People were lying around on the grass, throwing
the frisbee around, as if they had no idea that just a few feet
away, there were men lurking in the shadows for sex. But
this place, the Ramble, it's like a forest practically, near the
lake with the boats that the goyim row around. And there
were people on the boats, it was late afternoon, after mincha
time, and they were laughing and having fun. I was wearing
my baseball cap and jeans, and also I should mention that I
had taken off my tzitzis as soon as I entered the woods, and
I put them in my bag, because chas v'sholem someone might
see them on me, they would see and it would be mores ayin

to'evah – abomination, taboo
mincha – afternoon prayers
mores ayin – something that appears improper

again. I felt bad taking off my tzitzis, because of course they are there to remind us, to keep us away from exactly the sexual averas I was trying to commit, and I saw how right that was, but I was too far gone to be helped.

I met this man, in the Ramble, and he said I was good-looking and asked would I like to come with him. He wasn't old like the people in the bathhouse but he was older than me. Thirties, maybe. He looked like maybe he was Jewish, I thought, with dark hair and pale skin, and I thought at least he would be circumcised, and I know I shouldn't have gone with the man, but I went with him to a kind of secluded place where there were trees all around and no one could see us, not even the other men who were walking around the park. He felt me down there, and he said I was cute and I said thanks. And he leaned in to kiss me and I let him because after all that is what I came there for, to be with a man like this, and then he took off my baseball cap, really quickly, before I could stop him, and my payes kind of flopped down, and you know they're not very long, because it's not our minhag to keep the payes long like others do, but they were noticeable I guess because he asked me: "Are you Jewish?" And I said yes, because I learned never to deny, that to deny your yiddishkeit is among the worst sins, so I said it even though I didn't really want to as soon as I'd said it. And then he surprised me because he put his hand on my payes and he said, "Are you Chabad?" And I said, "What gives you that impression," which I know is kind of a funny way to say it but that's how I said it for some reason. And he

yiddishkeit – Jewishness

said, "You *are* Chabad! But you don't have a beard," he said.
And then he looked at my beard, you know, where it kind of
is, and he said, "I see," like it was some secret or something
that he had just discovered. And I didn't say anything but
just stood there.

Then he started talking like all of a sudden he was someone else, like he was possessed by a dybbuk or something
mamesh crazy. He said, "You know I grew up Chabad, I
was born frum, in a million years I never thought I'd end
up here." All of a sudden as he is saying this, now he sounds
like he is Chabad, mamesh with the accent and just the way
he was speaking to me. And he continues, "But you know
the Alter Rebbe said that everything is God, there is nothing
besides God, no place is devoid of Him, nowhere, not even
here." And all this time, Rebbe, he's undoing my clothing,
you know, taking off my shirt, and then taking off his. And
I'm just standing there because I never expected anything
like this and I'm astonished, and he says, "But you know,
the most important thing to understand about the Alter
Rebbe's words"—he said this as he took down my pants—
"is that everything that seems to be real is actually nothing,
ayin v'efes mamesh, because the world which seems to be
yesh is really just an extension of the Ein Sof, an extension
of God." By this time I was completely naked, and I was
aroused, and he got down on his knees in front of me and
put it inside his mouth. But somehow he continued speaking

dybbuk – spirit possession
ayin v'efes mamesh – absolutely void and empty
Ein Sof – the Infinite (God)

anyway, he said, "The union of opposites is the essence of *Chassidus*, to see that everything is God, even what we think of as evil, even this is God, in this moment, now, what I am doing to you, because there is nothing but God, anywhere, at any time, because everything is God. What do you think of that?" He looked up at me.

"I don't know," I answered, because I didn't know.

He told me to lie down, and I did, and he took off the rest of his clothes and lay on top of me. He said, "You see, you might think what you are doing now is evil, but it can't be, it's impossible for it to be, because everything is God, everything is the Ein Sof. There is no difference between the side of light and of shadow, do you understand?" All this as he was feeling me or kissing me or whatever, and I admit, I was aroused by him, and also afraid of what he was saying. He continued, "You know, the Alter Rebbe had what he called *avodah b'hipukh*, serving the kadosh boruch hu through the lowest of forms, because the highest was the lowest. And you know that before him, there were other Hasidim, and they would practice the greatest sins of the Torah in order to see that the Divine sparks reside even in the klippos hatmayos, even in the most fallen places—even here, do you understand?" I could only answer quietly, I guess, it's not that I didn't understand what he was saying, I understood perfectly the words he was saying, I just couldn't believe it, I couldn't believe what was happening, my body felt as if on fire, I thought mamesh that maybe it was a dream, or that this was the Satan himself, because of how he was twisting

Chassidus – Hasidism

the words of the Alter Rebbe, what he was saying and what
he was doing.

Then he lifted up my legs to my shoulders. I saw what he
was preparing to do, and thought to myself, that this could
not be true, I thought, it could not be so, and he said, "Do
you know who it was that first taught *avodah* through inversion, that the lowest is the highest?" And I whispered no, but
by then he was holding my legs up and pinning me to the
ground, and I could feel the ground, the soil and the grass,
cold underneath me, and he said, "Shabtai Zvi." And at
that moment he spit on his kli and on me, and he looked in
my eyes to see if I knew what he was talking about, and he
entered me, and I knew, because I had heard about Shabtai
Zvi, that he was a moshiach sheker and very evil, and so I
knew that this man was a rasha, but I couldn't say anything
because of the pain and the shock that I was feeling, but
Rebbe, what he said about the Tanya and Hashem was
right, so was this right too? Was this the truth? And he said,
panting almost, "I'm going to bring you to Hashem!" And
Rebbe, I had no idea it would be this painful, what they
do all the time, but he was saying, "Become your opposite,
become your opposite," over and over, and I said, or cried
sort of, "What do you mean," and he said: "Up, down, yesh,
ayin, a sinner, a Hasid, a man, a woman."

And I had in my head an image when he said that,

Shabtai Zvi – heretical messiah Sabbatai Zevi
kli – tool; euphemism for penis
moshiach sheker – false messiah
rasha – evildoer

of Chava with the snake, of woman being the source of temptation, which we learned about in yeshiva, that Lilith and Chava and all women were of the sitra achra, but as he said it I felt him so deep inside of me and I realized it was true: that I *was* that, I was a woman, and I believed him, or my body believed him, and the words of the nachash were the words of the moshiach, and in that instant I switched over and something changed and I said, "Yes," and he said, "A woman," and I said, "Yes," and he, it was like he was joining into me, and I don't know what had come over me, it wasn't shichvat zera but it was something greater, holier than anything I had felt, I realized: it was the female waters, from within me, and I was shouting yes, yes, and I was releasing the waters, mamesh, and I moaned a sound I had never heard before, and he kept saying it, like davening almost, a rasha, a hasid, a woman, a man, and he finished and his seed was inside me, and he was part of me, and we collapsed together, and we lay together, and I knew there would be no tshuva from this.

And then I passed out. I wasn't asleep, but neither was I awake. I had a dream that I was Yakov Avinu, that I was wrestling with a man—you know we learned in shiur that the Torah doesn't say angel, it just says *Ish*, he wrestled with an Ish—and in my dream I was like Yakov, like the holy Zohar says, but letting him win, this rasha, this tzaddik, this Shabtai Zvi. I looked over at him lying next to me and I hit

shichvat zera – spilling of seed
Yakov Avinu – Jacob the patriarch
ish – man

him with a rock and blood came from his head. Only then the blood was coming from my head, only it wasn't blood, the red had turned to white, like the sweetening of the dinim. But then I awoke again and my zera was on the ground, and the man was no longer there. I thought, did I kill him, was this a dream? But no, I was naked and dirty and in pain, as if I felt him still inside of me, so at least some of it was real. I gathered my clothes before anyone could see. I went back to the public part of the park, with the people in their goyishe little boats, with no idea what was happening or what was true, but I knew, Rebbe, I knew.

In telling this to you, Rebbe, I have to say, maybe I've changed my mind. I came to you to do tshuva, to beg your forgiveness and G-d's, but I don't know even what that means anymore or if even you can hear me, or if even you still exist. Perhaps the klippos I encountered were really the klippos nogah, and were uplifted, unified, in this way; maybe I had the z'chus to taste the me'ein olam haba, that is the aspect of moshiach, like the tzaddikim with their bittul hayesh except greater, deeper, because it is found in materiality, and from such a place, Rebbe, how is one to do tshuva, how is one to return to Hashem, whom one can never leave?

klippos nogah – "shells" that can be illuminated
me'ein olam haba – taste of the world to come
bittul hayesh – self-negation

THE ENLIGHTENMENT

OF RABBI YOSEF OF CHERNOBYL

1. WATER

In the year 5583, which among the nations is reckoned as 1823, Rabbi Yosef Duvid, the ninth grandson of the famous Rabbi Menachem Nachum of Chernobyl (may the memory of the righteous be for a blessing) journeyed to the Land of Israel largely out of desperation. Many Hasidim spoke of his journey with reverence, assuming it to be a holy pilgrimage, like those of many sages before him. But in fact, it was an escape.

All of R. Yosef's brothers, three older and two younger, were by now established with wives and families—some even with small communities forming around them. Many held court, where pious followers petitioned them for advice, counsel, or maybe a segulah or blessing from the rebbe. But R. Yosef, though already twenty-six years of age, had neither followers nor wife. He had refused the shiduchim that were offered him over the years, and lived still at his father's house. Moreover, although technically a rabbi, owing to his prodigious learning and a formal ordination by his father, R. Yosef did not seek followers, and few sought him. His name was known only because of his lineage and the fame of his grandfather, the great sage known by the title of his holy book, the *Meor Einayim*, as well as the lavish court of his father and the growing renown of his brothers. R. Yosef was alone and adrift, even if outwardly he projected wisdom, even holiness.

Of the teachings contained in secret books, R. Yosef was a master. He had immersed himself, even more than his brothers, in the teachings of his grandfather, of the Baal Shem Tov, and of other Hasidic masters. More than that, he learned from everyone, conversing even with those whose company he was warned not to keep, reading even some foreign books, with their philosophies and speculations, and with ideas that seemed to unite the disparate worlds, if such a thing were possible. Yet all this, he knew, was but the outer garment of true *yirah*, true fear of heaven. R. Yosef had yearned for the kind of love that his grandfather had known: that burning enthusiasm, *hitlahavus*—to be aflame with love of God. But he had never actually felt such a flame in his heart, never the consummation of intimacy, and never the all-consuming passion that, in its fire, annihilates the self and brings the soul to union. He felt as if he were the young sage Akiva, watching scholars through a window, forever at a certain remove, or as if he could describe a banquet, down to every ingredient of every dish, but could not, for some reason, taste the delicacies that others effortlessly enjoyed.

And then the dream came. In it, R. Yosef saw a vision of the *sneh*, the burning bush, in which the Holy One first spoke to Moshe. The bush was in the desert, surrounded by spacious horizons of sand and rock. It was not a place R. Yosef could identify, but he felt he knew it intimately. The fire leapt out from the bush, and R. Yosef jumped back in fear. And then the bush spoke to him, in the voice of Rabbi Nachman of Breslov, who had journeyed to the Land of Israel over twenty years ago. "Why do you recoil from the holy fire?" the voice asked. "Only he who is willing to be destroyed can be filled with the fire of the Holy One. Only because this bush burns, is it able to endure." R. Yosef realized, still in his dream, that he must make the same pilgrimage as Rabbi Nachman; only then would he overcome the obstacles that stood between him and his goal of complete annihilation in the fire of Divine love.

When he awoke the next morning, however, R. Yosef began to doubt. Was he really running to God, or was he running away? Flight was hardly the proper motive for a holy journey. And so R. Yosef put off his plans, telling no one of his dream of Rabbi Nachman. He continued, Shabbos after Shabbos, to sing and dance in the court of his father as if he were filled with joy. He spoke words of Torah and learned from more holy books in the yeshiva; for a time, he continued as before. Gradually, however, R. Yosef grew restless. Restless, and embarrassed, ever more acutely aware of his peculiarity, and wondering if people were beginning to whisper, in kitchens and market stalls, about him. Eventually his desire to leave grew stronger than his reservations about a pilgrimage undertaken for the wrong reasons. And gradually, a true yearning began to arise: not so much for the sacred sites of the holy land, but for the desert where he had stood in the dream. There was something at once familiar and foreign about it, both threatening and inviting.

Once R. Yosef had announced his intention to his father

and to the community, leaving had been a simple matter. Arranging the trip had cost R. Yosef all the money he had, as well as funds raised by his father, but it was not complicated to arrange. On the contrary, the pilgrimage was regarded as the answer to the questions that had swirled around R. Yosef for years. Still the community whispered about him, but now they whispered things like, *he is like the Nazir—a renunciate* and *what z'chus to be in the company of such a tzaddik.* Moreover, many Hasidim close to the Meor Einayim had settled in the Land of Israel, clustered primarily in Tiberias; R. Yosef's father felt such a connection to the town that he had based his own surname on its Hebrew name, Tveria. Perhaps, it was said, such journeys would hasten the coming of redemption. And so passage was secured, and within a few months of the dream R. Yosef found himself, on a humid summer evening, in Tiberias, the holy city of water.

* * *

The holy community of Tiberias lived in a fly-infested slum on the swampy shores of a stagnant lake. So, this is the sea of Galilee, R. Yosef thought—hardly a sea at all. He knew, despite his father's enthusiasm, that Tiberias was not to be his ultimate destination. But the journey had been arduous, and he had taken ill; now he was exhausted, hungry, and in need of rest. R. Yosef's family had sent word of their son's journey, and when he arrived in Tiberias, the young scion of the Meor Einayim was treated as an honored guest. Soon enough, Shabbos came around, and R. Yosef was requested to give a *vort* after a modest dinner of fish stew.

"Everything is one: Torah, Israel, God, the world," R. Yosef spoke in Yiddish, quoting from his grandfather as he had many times before. *"Altz iz Gott un Gott iz altz.* All is God. This is the fundamental truth, the kernel of the matter— and the basis of the teachings of the Holy Zohar, and the Holy Ari, and the Holy Baal Shem Tov—which my grandfather, the Meor Einayim, may the memory of the righteous be a blessing for us all, sought to elucidate in his teachings. For many generations this Torah remained concealed," R. Yosef continued, "but now in our days, the gates are opened and the inner light shines to all those who see."

R. Yosef looked around the table at the dozen or so Hasidim who were standing around it in dingy, yellowed shirts under threadbare black coats. The room was hot, and smelled equally of thick stew and sweat. People are starving here, R. Yosef thought as he gazed at the haggard faces around him. I should have stayed home.

Late that first Shabbos night, there was singing and even dancing at the tisch, but, R. Yosef felt, they sang the zmiros largely out of rote, continuing with the wordless niggunim just long enough so they could not be accused of lacking enthusiasm. He tried to look into the eyes of the Hasidim, but few would meet his gaze in the lamplight. The walls were made of blue-gray stone, and mildew seemed to cling to them, its stench mingling with the smell of sweat and the odor of the swamps just outside. Mosquitoes hovered every-

vort – short homily

where, and the Hasidim seemed chiefly preoccupied with swatting them against their red and bitten necks. Their shirt collars were stained with perspiration.

Amid this half-hearted celebration, R. Yosef remembered a time when, as a little boy, he had sat at his father's side as the pious shouted, sang, and danced. One time, after the singing had died down, his father said, "To be holy is kadosh, which has within it *y'kod esh*, to be burning with fire. Yossele, remember always to be on fire."

After about an hour of singing and another vort from the rebbe, the tisch was over. Several of the Hasidim had fallen asleep already, right at the table, with crumbs of bread still lodged in their beards. Others had left without a word. R. Yosef remained at the table as his host's wife began cleaning up the mess. Three other men were there, in varying states of sleep. One, a certain Reb Zissel, stirred, and mumbled in Yiddish, "Reb Yosef of Chernobyl, you teach secrets to little children."

"Perhaps it is the keeping of secrets which makes them like children," R. Yosef replied.

"Sometimes," responded Reb Zissel, "knowing secrets is worse than not knowing them."

R. Yosef sipped a dreg of wine from his cup.

By then, Reb Zissel had already fallen back asleep.

* * *

The days passed. R. Yosef gradually rested from his journey, and soon it would be time to move onward to Jerusalem, where distant relatives awaited his arrival. He had grown closer to Reb Zissel; R. Yosef had met his wife, Ritl, and little Chana had played on his lap. This was the life that R. Yosef had been denied, and the truth pained him. Yet the space in his heart made room for the Holy One, so was it not appointed for a purpose? R. Dov Ber, the Maggid of Mezritch, had taught that a broken heart is the prerequisite for becoming an abode for the Divine Presence, who Herself wanders in exile. Like the fragile voice of prophecy, the broken heart of the pious—not the fire or the noise—is where She is found. Was this not, too, the teaching of R. Nachman, only ten years R. Yosef's senior: that nothing is so whole as a broken heart?

A few days before R. Yosef was set to depart, Reb Zissel guided him through the steep hills above Tiberias so he could visit the graves of certain tzaddikim. The Holy Ari wrote that these sites contained great power: if one prostrated oneself on the graves, recited the right psalms and magical formulae, then he could unite with the soul of the departed. Nowadays, R. Yosef knew, we lack the merit to accomplish this task and can only pray to the holy soul of the tzaddik for help. Still, there was merit in making the journey. Presently they arrived at the grave of Rabbi Hutzpit the Interpreter, who was martyred by the Romans, perched on the side of a deep canyon. The grave was painted white, littered with the remains of candles and oils brought there by pious men and women praying for help, healing, or protection. And so R. Yosef began to pray to the holy neshama of Rabbi Hutzpit both in silence and aloud, so that Reb Zissel could hear his words; so that R. Yosef could, for a moment, not be alone in his aloneness.

"What have I done with my life?" R. Yosef began, inspired by the confessional prayers of Rabbi Nachman. "I have tried to serve heaven, in my way, in a way that would be mine, that only I could follow. I have tried, each day, to find a moment that is significant, that touches the life of the world. But I find I have accomplished nothing, built nothing, created nothing of note. What talents I have, I have squandered. What gifts I have, I have spent. If the Holy One were to take me today, I would feel only satisfaction— not because I have done the work I was apportioned, but because extinguishment would be no different."

Reb Zissel listened and looked out at the valley, the foliage dry and brown in the heat of summer. Then he said in reply, "My friend, I have found only that there is comfort to be found each day, solace in the simplest of objects. I watch my Chaneleh play with the lid of a pot, or an apple, and they are like the jewels of the kingdom for her. She is fascinated by them, and content. And so I too am satisfied with these simple things. When we have enough bread, or good air to breathe, fresh water from the lake, each gift from the *kadosh boruch hu*. Not in a boastful way, Yosef, but with *anoveh*, the humility that it is not my lot to bring the Messiah—only to live generously, obey the laws of the Torah, and recognize the good of what is."

R. Yosef said nothing. Such sentiments had once been true for him, when he was younger, entranced by the miracle of pine cones. Even now they warmed R. Yosef's heart, but now with an admixture of despair that even these simple joys seemed to be denied him.

"What have you come here to seek?" Reb Zissel asked after a time.

"Why do you think I am seeking something?" asked R. Yosef.

"Everyone who comes here is seeking something," Reb Zissel answered. "Living in exile, seeking home."

"*Nafshi cholas ahavasecha*," answered R. Yosef, quoting the psalm: *My soul thirsts for your love.*

"How would you know it if you felt it?"

To this, R. Yosef had no reply.

"When a man is in love," Reb Zissel continued, understanding without speaking, "it is both inexplicable and needs no explanation. We cannot prove what love is. There is no cloud of love that men can see with their eyes. But we know that love exists, because the pull of love is so strong, it cannot be denied. So it is with God."

The two walked onward for a moment.

"However," he continued, "when a man only yearns for love, and does not feel his love returned, he creates tales about his beloved. Perhaps she looks this way; she likes this and hates that. He replaces reality with these tales. And if another man should tell him differently—maybe your beloved has brown hair and not black!—he will argue forcefully: No! In this way, discord rises in the world, and the man himself becomes estranged from true love, which is open to every possibility.

"On your path," Reb Zissel continued, again with his

piercing gaze, "there can be no *ahavas hashem*. You will always doubt yourself until you come to know love. And yet, this you will not allow. You love your love so much, you will not let yourself experience it. You are trapped, my friend. I fear that you may contribute much to the world but suffer in order to do so."

R. Yosef wanted to cry, but did not want to say more. The two walked onward until the sun was beginning to set, then returned to the town. By the time R. Yosef was alone, the tears had already been swallowed.

2. AIR

Before turning south to Jerusalem, R. Yosef made a short journey to the mystical city of Safed, city of air. Once Safed had been the center of Kabbalah in the Holy Land, and even now, though this was no longer the case, still there were those who tended the graves of the Ari and his circle and who walked in the footsteps of Rabbi Shimon Bar Yochai, the great master of mysteries, and unlike Tiberias, Safed was home to a large community of some 5,000 souls. In particular, R. Yosef had heard stories about a singular *mekubbal* possessed of powers to heal and to tell the future, and also, it was said, to read minds. And so, with trepidation as well as yearning, R. Yosef ascended into the rarefied air of Safed, with its twisting alleyways, ancient synagogues,

ahavas hashem – love of God
mekubbal – Kabbalist

and holy gravesites, its small Jewish community clinging to the side of a hill.

After making the requisite pilgrimages to the gravesites of the Ari, the Ramak, and other sages buried in the grave-yard, R. Yosef plunged into the icy mikva of the Ari, fed by a small spring inside a cave just above the cemetery. In the heat of the summer, the waters were delightfully refreshing, and R. Yosef had the place almost to himself. For a moment, he enjoyed a reprieve from his thoughts and worries; he was alone, and felt purified.

The Kabbalist's study was not far from the mikva. R. Yosef had sent advance word of his arrival, and when he knocked on the blue-painted door of the Kabbalist's yeshiva, he was greeted quickly. He bent down under the low archway and was brought directly before the great mekubbal of Safed, seated in his private study with an assistant to his right, who was holding a cup of tea. Seated—and yet, it seemed to R. Yosef, hovering, as if not quite of this world, as if the mekubbal were a disembodied head, a mind only partly attached to a body. R. Yosef paid his respects, and the mekubbal replied with a blessing of R. Yosef's noble grandfather. There was then a pause, which R. Yosef understood as an invitation for him to state his request.

"I have come to the holy land in search of wisdom—or perhaps solace," he began. "In my youth, I used to think that the enlightenment of which the secret books teach was a matter of knowledge: that there was a secret answer to the old rebbes' questions, not written in books, but passed down from master to disciple. But in the court of my father,

I came to understand that to be enlightened was to experience the closeness of the Holy One through whatever means: through prayer, ecstasy, study, meditation. I have had small glimpses. Once, during meditation, I had a sense that everything around me was operating according to certain laws, as if they were all watches that had been wound by the *Borei Olam*, only the Creator was living in the watches, too, and breathing through every tick and tock." R. Yosef paused. "I am sure that my grandfather had this experience many times over, many times more powerful, in complete *devekus* with Hashem. And so I thought, this must be enlightenment, this—this way of being at and in a certain moment. It was sweet like the taste of honey. But eventually, it passed. *Ratzo v'shov*, as the sages say, running and returning—only, it would rarely return, and frequently I would fall into melancholy. My mind understands but my heart does not."

The Kabbalist listened, his eyes closed.

"One time, not long after I became a bar mitzvah," R. Yosef continued, "I was walking in the countryside near my home, and I became lost. Quickly I grew terrified—of bandits, or of beasts, or maybe of the night itself. Yet in my terror there was a clarity. And I knew that I *didn't* believe. In my heart of hearts, I didn't—my mind knows that all is one, but my neshama still doesn't, because if it did, I wouldn't feel so alone, so scared. But I seek your counsel, for I feel lost on my quest, unsure even of what I am looking for."

There was a long pause. The Kabbalist's eyes were still

Borei Olam – Creator of the World
devekus – spiritual connection (lit. "cleaving")

closed, so R. Yosef's gaze wandered over his cluttered bookshelves, packed with yellowed manuscripts piled one atop
the other. The Kabbalist furrowed his brow and finally
stirred to answer.

"You think your intuitions and feelings are G-d!" he
suddenly shouted, causing R. Yosef to shudder. "You know
nothing, Yosef of Chernobyl. One may have a gross sensation of the Shechinah simply after drinking l'chayim. What
you mistake to be the presence of G-d, what you dare to
presume, is merely the lowest of the rungs. And I see in
your heart that there is *safek* there, that you are even unsure
if there are rungs, if the supernal worlds are real. You are
wrong, Yosef of Chernobyl! Worse than wrong—this is
the kernel of evil. That which we cannot perceive is real.
That which we experience is illusion, only the surface of
things. The secrets of God are not in the excitement of your
emotions, Reb Yosef. They are in the esoteric truths of the
supernal."

R. Yosef was stunned by the rebuke.

"Do you really believe," the Kabbalist continued, "that
the great secrets of the Kabbalah are merely elaborations of
what you yourself have already experienced? Your grandfather spoke only the truth that the masses could understand,
he knew full well that it was but the surface of the matter. All
may be One, but the thirty-three pathways, the ten sefirot
in the four worlds, the two-hundred-and-sixteen intentions,
these are what determine the course of events in this lowest

safek – doubt

of worlds, this abominable shell of flesh, and he who transgresses against them shall perish just as is foretold. You say you seek wisdom but you are trapped on the lowest level. You are in error, Yosef of Chernobyl.

"Look at this cup of tea," he continued, holding it aloft. "What is its essence? Only the holy letters bring sense and meaning to things. Without the Divine letters there is only the unintelligibility of animals. The sefirot operate independently of your supposed intuition. Do not believe that you can know all there is, or that in a few flashes of devekus you can know the passageways of the supernal. You think that through your moments of clarity you understand the flow of the shefa? You may intuit this or that, Reb Yosef, but you cannot know the ways of the Ancient of Days.

"And anyway," the Kabbalist said, slowing down his words, "this is not really what you seek. You seek to change your sorrow into joy, and this is not within your power. I can lead you into the locked garden, I can teach you secrets of repair. But this is not what you truly want."

That was the last thing the Kabbalist said. He began to cough rather violently, and R. Yosef took his leave. He returned to Tiberias, and the next day, traveled southward to Jerusalem.

3. FIRE

On the holy fast of Tisha B'Av, on which the pious mourn the destruction of the Temples, R. Yosef was in Jerusalem. Here,

Hasidim were a small minority of the Jewish population: most were Sephardim, as well as Jews from foreign lands, and even Karaites and *minim* with whom one was forbidden to mingle. R. Yosef was one among many on pilgrimage, or in trade, or in some other state of temporary placelessness—and this, to him, was preferable. He had lodged with a *sofer* named Reb Yehuda Leyb, who by day made scrolls for *mezuzos* and in the evening copied manuscripts of the Kabbalah that were unknown even to R. Yosef. Reb Yehuda was twice R. Yosef's age, yet they spoke as equals, talking long into the night of mysteries R. Yosef had not heard expounded upon before: of the triple-trunked tree that from beyond the garden wall appeared to be three trees, but from within the orchard was seen to be but one; or of the Shechinah incarnated variously across the centuries, even as a young maiden. At times it seemed to R. Yosef that Reb Yehuda indulged overly in speculation, expounding on the *netzach* of *netzach* of *atzilus* and the *keter* of *malkhut* of *briyah* and all the rest. Yet there were other times when he would utter something extraordinary: how, in the world to come, the Torah of the Knowledge of Good and Evil, with its distinctions and prohibitions, would be replaced by the Torah of the Tree of Life, in which all differences were effaced; or how the Most High took delight in the boldness of women and men—how defiance was in fact service, since it affirmed the Divine in everything. Often these teachings were given over in the name of a certain "Rabbi Adam,"

minim – sectarians

sofer – scribe

but Reb Yehuda would say little more about him, and when R. Yosef would press for further explanations, Reb Yehuda seemed always to change the subject.

On the eve of Tisha B'Av, Reb Yehuda Leyb and some other Hasidim chanted *kinos* on a rooftop in the city. From where they sat, they could see the gold dome of the Ishmaelites on the Temple Mount, the gray dome of the Edomites to the north, and the many smaller domes of the Jewish quarter around them. They heard from within the ruins of the Hurva synagogue the sound of *Eicha* being read. The time came for R. Yosef to speak, and he opened in this way:

"The *beis hamikdash* was the connecting point, the place of meeting between *shamayim* and *aretz*. It was, as my grandfather of blessed memory would teach, the place where we saw what is always true, that every stone is filled with holiness, filled with G-d. Here the concealed was revealed. But we forgot. We forgot the meaning of the beis hamikdash and took it for granted, we lost the love, the spark, the desire for the kadosh boruch hu, which was the source of the kedusha, the aspect of the sacred *yichud*, reflected in the union of the *kruvim* over the *aron* in the *kodesh kedoshim*. And when one lover turns away, the other lover turns away, which is what Hashem did when Bnei Yisroel turned away from Him, the holy Shechinah departed.

kinos – dirges
Eicha – Book of Lamentations
shamayim – heaven/sky
aretz – earth
aron – ark
kodesh kedoshim – holy of holies

"So now we are brokenhearted," R. Yosef continued. "But even now, as Rebbe Nachman teaches, the broken heart is our most faithful companion. Because when we are brokenhearted, we know that we are brokenhearted, we feel the heart, and even though we know that there is nothing but the kadosh boruch hu, right here and now, still there is this yearning. This is the holy yearning. This is the secret of Tisha B'Av: that the brokenheartedness is also G-d. And even—even when there is not yearning, even when there is only a lack, a part of us is crying for that connection. Even if we cannot hear it, we are yearning to yearn. And this too is yearning."

R. Yosef looked around the room. He caught Reb Yehuda Leyb's eye. "Rebbe, may I expound for a moment on what you have just said?" Reb Yehuda asked.

"By all means."

"I heard in the name of my master Rabbi Adam, may the memory of the righteous be for a blessing, the following teaching," Reb Yehuda Leyb began, his voice deeper than R. Yosef's and with the distinctive accent of his native Poland. "When is love greatest? When it is about to depart. When a man is about to go on a journey, the night before he leaves is the sweetest, most passionate night he spends with his wife. Because he knows he will be gone. And that sweetness lasts up until the actual moment of separation. Reb Yosef has said that the churban of Tisha B'Av came about because we lost the yearning. But he has also said that we never lose the yearning. How can both be true? Because in fact Tisha B'Av is the moment of the greatest love between God and His people. The lowest is the highest; the most abased is the most exalted. It is on this night that, on one level, the Shechinah leaves us, and on that level, the desire is the strongest, the kruvim unite in the greatest rapture. But on another level, this devotion and love is revealing what is always happening, even at this very instant, mamesh at this moment: the breaking of the vessels and the shattering of our hearts—and also the repair of the vessels and the revelation of joy, which is born on Tisha B'Av. At precisely the moment when we feel the farthest from G-d, that is when G-d is whispering in our ears, saying, 'Come closer, come closer, the voice of my beloved knocks at the door.' And then if we listen, we understand that *geula* is already here, seen through the eyes of *moshiach,* which is the aspect of expansion; the Shechinah is already united with the kadosh boruch hu, the *tikkun* is accomplished. There is no need for demarcation; freedom is the secret of the Torah of the Tree of Life. The *heshek* of the kruvim is not distant from us, despite the external world; because on the level of moshiach, malkhus is already in wholeness, already surrounding and filling, as your grandfather said, from G-d's point of view, which is the aspect of geula, of redemption. And so indeed the secret is that there is no secret at all, only the act of veiling, of concealing and revealing, as in this realm, so in the other, where the concealment increases the yearning, the heshek, when it is revealed and opened, as it is written. Indeed, Rabbi Yosef, sometimes the concealment is such that darkness overwhelms us, and

heshek – desire

on this level we are indeed lost and abandoned and a great evil threatens us. Yet at precisely such a time, the redemption appears, *domeh dodi litzvi*, my beloved is like a deer, and he says *kumi lach*, rise up, *et hazamir higiyah*, the winter is over, the time for singing has come."

And at that moment Reb Yehuda Leyb and the other men sang with special intensity, even songs that R. Yosef did not know, love songs for the Shechinah, some in a foreign tongue; they sang rejoicing in her, until many were moved to tears of joy, of celebration, of sacred yearning and heshek for one another and for God. It was as if R. Yehuda Leyb's words were the essence even of the *Meor Einayim*, but the secret essence which R. Yosef's grandfather could not reveal to the world. The singing continued in this way for almost an hour, until finally the men dispersed, filled with joy and love, though maintaining silence outwardly since it would be unseemly to reveal it on such a night.

Shortly after midnight, R. Yosef awoke from a dream. He had been running through a corridor, but when he reached the end, he realized he'd been running in the opposite way from what he had intended. His father was there, admonishing him, and R. Yosef turned around to run back, yet when he turned, his father was somehow still facing him. There was a peculiar light in the corridor, as if it were lit from outside translucent walls. Finally, in anger, he thoughtlessly punched his fist against the corridor's wall, made of pale Jerusalem stone; he cried out, and awoke.

On the other side of the room they shared in Reb Yehuda Leyb's modest dwelling, Reb Yehuda was fast asleep, and snoring. The night air admitted of no release; it was as warm now as it had been in the daytime, R. Yosef thought. A single fly flew in circles around the room. R. Yosef noticed that his hands had moved, unconsciously, below his waist; he instinctively moved them away, as he had been taught. But in that fear there was contraction, the imposition of lines. Was this righteousness or error, R. Yosef wondered. If there is no *tameh* there can be no *tahor*; nothing profane, nothing sacred. But then, R. Yosef pondered the words of Reb Yehuda Leyb, that such distinctions were illusory, that redemption was at hand; or had already occurred; or was occurring at this very moment! R. Yosef wanted to strip off his bedclothes, feast on honeyed cakes, and awaken the pious from their slumber. Perhaps the messiah born on this day will be the one who redeems us from the delusion of the messiah! The fly circled in the room as R. Yosef did or did not fall back asleep.

The next morning, R. Yosef felt a lightness within him. It was not that his yearning had been answered; it was that the need for an answer had been relinquished. Now the world is as it is, R. Yosef thought to himself as he recited the morning benedictions. As he placed his fringes on his body, caked with sweat and grime, he banished nothing from his mind. As he relieved himself and recited the blessing honoring the Creator, he admitted all, his body bare before God. This filth is that which you have ordained, R. Yosef prayed. *Bashomayim uvo'oretz, ein oid*, that in heaven and earth there

tameh – impure
tahor – pure

is nothing else—how many times have I heard discourses on these words? But never did I understand: that if there is nothing else, there is no inside or outside, there is no backward and forward, and on the holiest planes, no permitted and forbidden.

With those words, R. Yosef's eyes were opened and he felt as though he were falling.

* * *

The rest of the morning was spent in a palace of fire. The very pores on R. Yosef's skin seemed to comprehend the truth of God's beneficence, the extension of His will into even foreign realms—no, not even, precisely, in the way most sanctified—into the places that the fools label as darkness. But not only the fools—everybody! It is a natural thing. That which is beloved is beloved, that which is abhorred, abhorred. Nothing could be more elemental. But this was the illusion. Everything was consumed in this blaze: solids and liquids, ecstasies, contraries. And yet R. Yosef was externally pacific, sitting on the floor as required, pretending to recite more dirges of mourning. He spoke of this to no one, not even to Reb Yehuda—especially not to him.

That afternoon, Reb Yehuda took R. Yosef to the mikva. It is forbidden to bathe on Tisha B'Av, but the mikva is an exception since it is not bathing in the ordinary sense. Because it was a hot summer day, the mikva was very crowded. It was a natural spring, located outside the walls of the city, near the waters of Shiloach. There were men, boys, adolescents—all fasting, and mostly silent. Some of the men were hairy, and some were smooth. R. Yosef averted his eyes, as was his habit—but why, he thought to himself, and raised his head. And so when it came R. Yosef's turn to enter the mikva, his eyes met those of another man about to enter. Their gaze froze together for a moment, then released. R. Yosef entered and then the man entered. The water was deliciously cool, and R. Yosef could not help letting out a sigh. Had anyone heard? The man next to him seemed not to have heard a thing. R. Yosef washed his face briefly, then immersed seven times, as was his custom. On one of the immersions, he accidentally brushed against the other man. He tried not to lose count of his immersions.

When R. Yosef emerged from the mikva, he noticed the man looking back at him. Indeed, now it seemed everyone was looking at everyone else, though of course this was not the case. R. Yosef remembered where he was, and that on the hills on which he was now looking out, idolatrous rites were carried out by the Canaanites and the Israelites who mingled with them. Abominations were performed, ceremonies and sacrifices. Were these, too, in service of the Exalted One? Could it be possible?

Upon leaving, Reb Yehuda said the following to R. Yosef as they walked on the way: "That which conceals is that which reveals, Reb Yosef. This you still do not seem to understand. Come and learn. The Most High cannot be known, cannot be manifest in any way, except through His tikkunim, which has the aspect of garments. The *or* must become `*or*, the light must take on a skin. In exactly this way, the only means for revelation is concealment."

R. Yosef remained silent, pondering whether Reb Yehuda Leyb had read his thoughts, whether he was wise or a fool—or a *rasha*.

The two stopped walking along the way, and stood for a moment on the pathway outside the city walls. Reb Yehuda then continued: "The reverse is also true. That which you seek, the most esoteric, the most hidden, is also the most revealed. The *bifnim* is the *panim*—the inside is the face, the essence is precisely and none other than exactly what is present, in this garb, at this instant."

R. Yosef moved to interrupt, but Reb Yehuda refused him. "There is more," he continued. "As it is said in the Idra, when the face is turned from on high, it cannot transmit the light to that which is below. The red-appled countenance of the rebellious one, contorted and compressed, neither receives from the light of the Ancient of Days, nor transmits mercies to that which is below. What is unwritten is this: as above, so below. When the face does not receive from below, it cannot be open to above. It is not, as some suppose, that a choice must be made between one and the other. The exact contrary is true. If there is a defect below, there will be a defect above. If there is a blockage below, there will be a blockage above."

R. Yosef said at last, "Is this not the way of the heretics? Of what meaning then is 'Thou shalt not have unequal measures. Thou shalt not walk in their ways'?"

And so Reb Yehuda answered him, with piercing eyes: "These and like transgressions are likewise: above, and below. Thus when there is true understanding above, there is true understanding below. *Sitrei arayot* are the *sharvit hamelech*; forbidden relations are the scepter of the king. Only the fool believes that when the force of love predominates, the force of sin will grow."

R. Yosef had spent his life measuring his love for the Holy One according to how faithfully he fulfilled the commandments, and with what measure of fervor he worshipped three times a day. R. Yosef knew that these were but external forms, of course, vessels to hold the holy *kavvanah* of the righteous ones, but nonetheless he held fast to them. He knew of the great heresies, those who had annulled or willfully violated the precepts, all for the sake, they said, of Heaven. Would that not be the greatest love, to transgress for the sake of Heaven? To elevate the sparks in the deepest abyss?

"What is it that you really seek?" asked Reb Yehuda Leyb.

"I seek wisdom," R. Yosef said.

"But why do you seek wisdom?"

R. Yosef paused for a moment, and said, "You know the answer, friend."

"You act as if to say a thing is no different than to know it. If such were the view of the Holy One, the world would not even exist. The only reason we are here is because He is speaking and not just thinking."

"I seek wisdom because I seek love, as you know."

"And that love—how would it be born from wisdom, even from enlightenment?"

"Because the root of wisdom is faith," answered R. Yosef.

"Faith!" Reb Yehuda Leyb shouted, for a moment reminding R. Yosef of the Kabbalist of Safed. "Cleaving to belief is the opposite of faith, R. Yosef. Faith is surrender, opening and receiving. Your path is one of distinctions everywhere."

The two men looked outward at the valley of the *tzalmavet*, the shadow of death. Suddenly a fly landed on Reb Yehuda's shoulder.

"Do you see this fly?" Reb Yehuda asked suddenly. "It is following its nature immediately. Its desire is neither shameful nor praiseworthy. And is it not beautiful?"

R. Yosef did not answer. Another fly landed on R. Yehuda.

"You are *ba'al-zvuv!*" R. Yosef cried. And he knew that it was true: that he who follows this path is the master of flies, because they do not disturb him.

"Yes," Reb Yehuda smiled as a fly landed on his forehead. "Because you must overcome even this."

"No!" R. Yosef cried, unable to tell if he was passing the test or failing it. Was he in love with God, or was he blocking God's love by restricting it to the sacred? Was this the truth of opposites? The two men stood face to face. R. Yosef thought that if he stood still enough, one of the flies would fly to him.

"Next week you must go to the desert at last," R. Yehuda said, unperturbed, "as you dreamt in your country. I have taught you all I can. You need a different kind of teacher."

At that moment, the man from the mikva passed R. Yosef and Reb Yehuda on the trail. He seemed to stare at R. Yosef

in a strange way, and R. Yosef was perplexed. Reb Yehuda
saw this.

"Why are you disturbed?" asked Reb Yehuda.

"That man was looking at me strangely."

"And?"

"Is that not enough?"

"It is not the whole truth."

R. Yosef stopped walking, as if to interrupt his momen-
tum would allow him to take the next step intellectually. "It's
almost as if they all know a secret, and I am about to learn
it," he said.

"They . . ."

"The ones who look at me this way. I notice it more and
more."

"And what is the secret?" asked R. Yehuda.

"I . . ."

"*What is the secret?*"

"I am ashamed for you to hear me say it."

"The more shame, the more truth."

"I think they are looking at me because they know." The
fear rose in R. Yosef's heart.

"They know . . ." Reb Yehuda began.

"That I am about to become enlightened."

4. EARTH

The next week, R. Yosef made his way to Hebron, the city of
earth. The heat of the summer was over; soon would come

the month of Elul with its penitential prayers in preparation for the Days of Awe. Now was the time for R. Yosef to make his final journey before returning homeward, before the weather grew too cold in the north.

In Hebron, R. Yosef lodged with a certain Reb Aharon Schorr, an acquaintance of Reb Yehuda's. Their interactions were pleasant enough, but they spoke only of simple matters. R. Yosef brought with him a note from Reb Yehuda, explaining everything to Schorr, and there was little to discuss, and no reason for delay. Soon enough, Schorr equipped the Hasid with enough water and food for a day's round trip, and sent him out east of the city, where there was a well-trodden path into the desert. R. Yosef set forth alone.

After about an hour in the wilderness, R. Yosef came upon a small spring, and near it a camel-hair tent. Out of the tent emerged a woman, her face and hair uncovered, her skin dark like Sheba's, her eyes seeming to burn without being consumed.

"Rabbi Yosef of Chernobyl, what are you doing in the desert?" she asked him in Hebrew.

R. Yosef stopped in his tracks, and stood still a few feet away from the woman. "How do you know who I am?" he asked haltingly, unused to conversing in the holy tongue.

"Answer my question."

And so he did, accustomed now to such extraordinary occurrences. "I came here to grow near to the Holy One, but now I am more confused than before. I don't know what is wisdom and what is folly. I feel I am on the verge of knowledge, but I am afraid."

"But I think you do already know, Rabbi Yosef of Chernobyl. I think your body knows but your mind cannot comprehend it. Where are you, Rabbi Yosef?"

"I—I am in the desert," he replied, looking beyond the spring to the rocks and hills of Judea. "I am in the wilderness. I do not know who you are."

"My name is Imma Eisha—that is what they call me here, because it resembles my true name."

"You are a sorceress. Or perhaps you are a *shed*."

Imma Eisha let out a hearty laugh. "Oh, Rabbi! You think I am a witch, and that your books are wise. But think about who wrote those books, and what they would make of you. Maybe you are right, Rabbi Yosef. You were warned about my wisdom for a reason. But every warning is an invitation to those who know it, Rabbi Yosef. From where do you think Rabbi Yehuda Leyb, and the others of his sect, learned their Torah?"

"What—how can you—"

"Rabbi Yosef," she continued, "what if there is no Holy One sitting in judgment, but only this world of magic, of circles and of earth. Filled with beings strange and terrible, and wonderful; changing always; full of desire and earth and water; full of kindness and cruelty that we inflict or withhold—we, not another. Is that not enough? This spring, it feeds all the springs of the Holy Land: the ones you have bathed in, the one your descendants will bathe in. This acacia tree speaks to all her sisters in the desert, including

shed – demon

one beneath which your own great-granddaughter will take shelter."

R. Yosef pondered this for a moment. "That is not my path," he said.

"Listen, Rabbi Yosef from Chernobyl," Imma Eisha continued. "There are many kinds of descendants. *Gilgulim*, dybbuks, children of the water. Look in your heart and in your body. Just because your intuition tells you something does not mean that it is so. Maybe it's only something you've believed for too long."

"But my yearning—"

"Rabbi Yosef of Chernobyl: There is nothing to realize. There is no truth to be grasped and deciphered, only one to be received. Your rabbis want to throw away, throw away, make the body, the soul submit to words and speculations. You want to be awakened, Rabbi Yosef, but they put you back into dreams. There is no judge withholding peace from you, Rabbi Yosef of Chernobyl. Your grandfather understood this, but knew he could not say it. So he led his people step by step."

"My grandfather was a tzaddik," said R. Yosef. The rocks, the desert, the spring seemed to swirl around the woman; all seemed on the verge of dissolution.

"Exactly, Rabbi Yosef. And why are the righteous described as enlightened—as light?"

"I don't know."

"But you do. And you know that this is not only your

gilgulim – reincarnations
dybbuks – spirit possessions

tradition. The Nazirites also have this, their saints pictured in halos. As do nations of which you are not aware. Why do you suppose that is?"

"I don't know," answered R. Yosef.

"But you *do* know. Stop trying to know or not know, and say what you know."

"Because they are radiating the light from within themselves," R. Yosef said hurriedly.

"That is right. And is it a trick, a special spell, perhaps?"

"No, it is their being," R. Yosef said.

"That is right," Imma Eisha replied. "And they know the secret that is not concealed. That there is no God because everything is God. They shine like the radiance of the firmament because all this is united already, concealed and revealed, these rocks and this sky are sufficient, the body and the imagination and the spring; and they know this. They lack nothing. There is no covenant, no promise, no reward, no punishment. No justice except that which we create with our holy effort. And you have known this, Rabbi Yosef of Chernobyl. When have you felt this?"

"When I was young, once I was swimming in the river with some of the other boys. And I went to get out and saw surrounding my shadow in the water, I saw rays of light shining in every direction. And I thought: it's true, it's true that I am the anointed one, it's true, and that is why I suffer. And then, after I thought that, I scolded myself for being so foolish and so silly and so proud—"

"But before that," Imma Eisha interrupted. "Before you elaborated with your stories of the Messiah and the redemption, before that—"

"There was the knowing you describe," said R. Yosef.

"So you do know, Rabbi Yosef of Chernobyl. You have known the mind of the Messiah, the one of whom your ancestors hesitate to speak. Though you have buried this knowledge, you have known the world to come."

"Yes," Rabbi Yosef admitted.

"And of course, now you know it does not pertain only to you. This knowledge is only Her, united with the Holy One and Its endlessness: Asherah, the happy one."

R. Yosef accepted this.

After a moment, Imma Eisha continued: "It is no coincidence, where and when you saw this sun-child. You experienced desire, and then you saw Her. In you. Ready to open, to receive, to unite with the rays of the sun."

"I have been afraid of admitting it."

"You feared you would be sundered from love if the Great Judge disappeared. But now you know that the opposite is true: in and out, dark and light, giving and receiving, it can never disappear, always breathing *ahava, yahava,* changing one; you know yourself in the acacia trees, in the water of the spring, the air in your lungs, in the eye that sees and the mind that knows. They recognize you, compassionate one."

R. Yosef was silent.

"The secret is only concealed by the act of concealment," said Imma Eisha. "This is the mystery of the kruvim. You can feel it if you wish, now that you know what it is."

And with the merest gesture, R. Yosef was able indeed to perceive it: he surrendered his body to the ecstasy of the holy of holies, of the krvuim atop the sacred ark, not merely resembling the sexual embrace, but enacting it, for it was one, and he breathed faster, and a sigh escaped his lips. Yes, he realized: the forbidden is the holy. There were no secrets anymore. "Oh," he sighed aloud.

"Yes, that's all it is," said the woman's voice. And R. Yosef heard it, and he shivered as if in intimacy, and his entire body was charged, and some part of him united with the spring and the tree, and he again sighed aloud, the roots penetrating him and the water flowing in the spring, deep underground, there to rest for two hundred years. And Imma Eisha said, "This is your way, Yosef Duvid of Chernobyl." And R. Yosef heard these words, and cried in astonishment, as no delight he had ever known had even approached this. It was lust and not lust; it was as if the rapture of union awakened every inch of his body, his feet tensed outward, the neck rolling back, the biceps strong and flexing, the seed within, the chest, eyes, he could feel it anywhere, on his lips, the kiss of the Divine.

And R. Yosef remembered. He was a child, sitting on his father's knee. His older brothers huddled around: once, they too had sat on Tateh's knee and heard the teachings of the Light of the Eyes. Now it was his turn.

"Yossele, it's your time to learn the great secret your grandfather taught to the world," his father said. His father knew everything. "But Yossele, it is a secret that each man must know for himself. You know how Mameh makes the cholent?"

"Yes, Tateh!" little Yosef answered.

"But could you make it yourself?"

Yosef did not know the right answer to say. He could, yes of course he could, but could he? What if he had to do it right now? Yosef felt nervous.

"No!" his father continued. "And neither could I! Even if Mameh listed all the steps and all the ingredients, we couldn't. So Yossele, I can only give you the recipe of this Torah. One day, maybe, when you're older, you'll taste the cholent."

"Yes, Tateh," Yosef said.

"The secret is that all this, everything you see, everything you think and feel, even all the terrible things that happen to our people—all this is the expansion of the Ein Sof, Yossele. The kadosh boruch hu is closer to us than we are ourselves. He's inside of us, inside each thought you have in your brain. And He's a pelican flying in *yenne velt!*"

Yosef burst into a peal of laughter. Then he thought for a moment, and asked a question: "But all the rasho'im and the bad things. Are they Hashem too?"

And Yosef's father was silent, because this question could not yet be answered for the boy.

"You're a smart boy, Yossele," his father said, and hugged him, and Yosef felt as loved as he ever had, as loved as a boy could ever be, as his father hugged him and held him and put his arms around him. He wanted never to stir from that embrace.

GLOSSARY OF HEBREW AND YIDDISH TERMS

Note: The definitions provided here are those according to traditional Judaism. Contemporary Jews often have different understandings of them.

Afikomen – Last matzo eaten at the Passover seder

Ahavat – Love

Ahavat Hashem/Ahavas Hashem – Love of God

Alter Rebbe – The founder of Chabad Hasidism

Aretz/Oretz – Earth

Aron – Ark

Aron Kodesh (pl. *Aronei Kodesh*) – Ark in a synagogue where Torah scrolls are kept

Asherah – Canaanite Goddess

Atzilut/Atzilus – Emanation

Avera – Sin

Avinu she-Bashamayim – God (lit. "Our Father in Heaven")

Avodah b'Hipukh – Service of God through inversion

Avodah Zara – Idolatry

Ayin v'Efes Mamesh – Absolutely void and empty

Baal Shem Tov – The founder of Hasidism

Ba'al Tshuva (pl. *Ba'alei Tshuva*) – One who takes on Jewish observance

Baruch/Boruch – Blessed

Baruch Hashem – Praise God

Bat Ayin – R. Avraham Dov of Avrich (1765–1840), who settled in Safed in 1830

Bat Kol – Divine voice (lit. "daughter of a voice")

Beit HaMikdash/Beis HaMikdash – The Temple

Beit Midrash/Beis Medrash – Study hall

Ben Azzai – Talmudic mystic who went insane

Bittul Hayesh – Self-negation

Bochurim – Male yeshiva students

Borei Olam – Creator of the World

Brachot/Bruchos – *Blessings*

Briyah – World of Creation

B'Seder – Okay

Chabad – The Lubavitch sect of Hasidim

Chalutz – Israeli pioneer

Chametz – Leavened food, prohibited on Passover

Chassidus – Hasidism

Chas v'Sholem – God forbid

Chava – Eve

Cholent – Stew served on the Sabbath

Churban – Holocaust, disaster

Dati – Religious

Devekus – Spiritual connection (lit. "cleaving")

Din (pl. *Dinim*) – Judgment

Dybbuk – Spirit possession

Eicha – Book of Lamentations

Ein Sof – The Infinite

Emunah – Faith

Frum – Religious

G-d – God (pious Jews do not write out the word "God")

Gabbai – Synagogue assistant

Gemara – A section of the Talmud

Genizah – Place for storage and burial of sacred texts

Geula – Redemption

Gilgulim – Reincarnations

Golem – Artificial human made by a Kabbalist

Goyim – Non-Jews

Goyishe – Non-Jewish

Halacha/Halachos – Jewish law(s)

Hashem – God (lit. "the Name")

Hasid – A follower of Hasidism

Hazzan – Cantor

Heikhalot – Heavenly palaces

Hesed – Sefirah of lovingkindness

Heshek – Desire

Hilonim – Secular Israelis

Ibbur – Spirit incubation

Ikkar/Ikker – Essence

Ish – Man

Kabbalat Shabbat – Friday night Sabbath service

Kadosh Baruch Hu/Kadosh Boruch Hu – God (lit. "the Holy One, Blessed be He")

Kahal/Kehilla – Congregation or community

Kashrut/Kashrus – Jewish dietary laws

Kavvanah – Intention

Kavvanot/Kavvanos – Kabbalistic meanings of prayer

K'deshim – Temple sex workers in Canaanite religions

Kedusha – Holiness

Keter – Sefirah of transcendence (lit. "Crown")

Kikayon – Mythical plant that sheltered Jonah in the desert

K'ilu – Like, as if

Kinos – Dirges

Kli – Tool, a euphemism for penis

Klippos – The "shells" or realms of evil

Klippos Hatmayos – "Shells" that are totally impure

Klippos Nogah – "Shells" that can be illuminated

Kodesh Kedoshim – Holy of holies

Kruvim – Cherubs

Lashon Hara/Loshon Hora – Gossip (lit. "evil speech")

L'Chayim – To life

Ma'aseh Merkavah – Early form of Jewish mysticism (lit. "workings of the chariot")

Maimar – Recorded speech or utterance

Malkhut/Malkhus – Sefirah of the Shechinah (Divine Presence)

Mama Loshen – Yiddish (lit. "mother tongue")

Mamesh – Really, actually (often used as a sort of verbal tic among Hasidim, like "like")

Maskil – Assimilated/rational Jew (a follower of the European Enlightenment)

Mechayeh – Wonderful thing (lit. "makes life")

Mechitza – Barrier separating men and women in traditional synagogues

Me'ein Olam Haba – A taste of the world to come

Mekubbal – Kabbalist

Mikva/Mikveh – Ritual bath

Mincha – Afternoon prayers

Minhag (pl. *Minhagim*) – Custom(s)

Minim – Sectarians

Minyan – Prayer quorum of ten men

Mishegas – Craziness

Mishkan – The biblical Tabernacle

Mishkov Zakhar – Homosexual acts (lit. "lying with a man")

Mishna/Mishnayot – The first part of the Talmud; also refers to individual portions therein

Mitzvah/Mitzvo (pl. *Mitzvot/Mitzvos*) – Commandment(s)

Mores Ayin – Something that appears improper

Moshiach – Messiah

Moshiach Sheker – False messiah

Motzei Shabbos – Saturday night

Nachash – Snake

Ner Tamid – Eternal light (lit in a synagogue)

Neshama – Soul

Netzach – Sefirah of endurance (lit. "Eternity")

Niddah – Laws of menstruation

Niggun – Wordless Hasidic melody

Nistar – Hidden

Nogah – Brightness, clarity

Ohel Moed – The biblical "tent of meeting"

Oleh (pl. *Olim*) – Immigrant(s) to Israel

Parsha – Weekly Torah portion

Payes – The distinctive side-curls of male Hasidim

Pesach – Passover

Pru Urvu – Be fruitful and multiply (the commandment to procreate)

Pshat – Surface, literal meaning

Rachamim/Rachmanus – Compassion, pity

Rasha (pl. *Rasho'im*) – Evildoer(s)

Rav/Rov – Rabbi

Rebbe – A term of intimacy and authority for a Hasidic
rabbi

Rebbeim – Rabbis

Rebbetzin – Rabbi's wife

Remez – Hint/allegory

Ribbono shel Olam/Ribbono shel Oilam – God (lit. "Master of
the Universe")

Sabbatean (Eng.) – Follower of the heretical messiah
Sabbatai Zevi

Safek – Doubt

Sefer – Book, especially a holy book

Sefirah (pl. *Sefirot*) – Emanation/aspect of God

Segulah – Amulet

Seichel – Sense

Shabtai Zvi – Seventeenth-century heretical messiah
Sabbatai Zevi

Shacharit/Shacharis – Morning prayers

Shamayim/Shomayim – Heaven, sky

Shammos – Synagogue "beadle"

Shechinah – Feminine Divine Presence

Shed (pl. *Shedim*) – Demons

Shefa – Divine flow

Shichvat Zera – Spilling of seed

Shiduchim – Arranged matches

Shiur – Lesson

Shlemut – Wholeness

Shomer(et) N'giah – Observant of chastity laws

Shtender – Book stand

Shuckling – Swaying in prayer

Shuk – Marketplace

Shul – Synagogue

Simcha – Joy, happy occasion

Sitra Achra – The "other side" or realm of evil

Sitrei Arayot – Laws of forbidden relations (lit. "The concealments/secrets of nakedness")

Sofer – Scribe

Sonei Yisroel – Enemies of Israel

Tahor – Pure

Tameh – Impure

Tanakh – Bible

Tanya – Central text of Chabad Hasidism

Tati/Tateh – Daddy

Tehillim – Psalms

Tiferet – Sefirah of beauty/compassion

Tikkun – Cosmic repair

Tikkun HaKlali – Set of psalms to "repair" sexual sin

Tisch – Hasidic Shabbat celebration

To'evah – Abomination, taboo

Tshuva – Repentance

Tzitzis – Fringes/fringed undergarment

Ussur – Forbidden

Vort – Short homily

Vayikra – Leviticus

Yakov Avinu – Jacob the patriarch

Yesh – Somethingness, reality

Yeshiva – Religious academy

Yetzer Hara/Yetzer Hora – Evil inclination, specifically the sexual urge

Yichud – Union, both sexual and spiritual

Yiddin – Jews

Yiddishkeit – Jewishness

Z'chus – Merit

Zmiros – Sabbath songs and hymns

ACKNOWLEDGMENTS

I started out writing fiction. This may come as a surprise to anyone familiar with my seven nonfiction books (plus two of poetry!) and numerous articles, but I think a lot of nonfiction writers start out that way. It's the dream, right? In fact, this collection had its genesis as a project for my MFA in fiction writing at Sarah Lawrence many years ago, and so the first thanks are due to the teachers and friends who were so supportive and attentive way back then, including Valerie Martin, Victoria Redel, Peter Cameron, Margot Livesey, Jonathan Vatner, and Alex Samets. Yet while I never stopped writing fiction, I was fortunate to find success in other work, and followed it where it led me. I may also have been reluctant to publish these stories, given their subject matter. But when Ayin Press came calling, I knew it was time for them to see the light of day. I have been so lucky to have worked with Eden Pearlstein, Tom Haviv, Penina Eilberg-Schwartz, and Moriel Rothman-Zecher on this project. They have made this book much better, juicier, and sharper, and have not allowed me to chicken out. Thank you. In the many years between Sarah Lawrence and Ayin, there have been many supportive readers, friends, and publishers of this work, including Rabbi Zalman Schachter-Shalomi z"l,

Toby Johnson, Sven Davisson, Joshua Henkin, Dan Friedman, Andrew Ramer, Jill Hammer, Steve Berman, Don Shewey, Larry Yudelson, Shir Meira Feit, Jordan Ellenberg, and Shoshana Cooper. Thank you, and deep bows to my friends and teachers in Jewish, Dharma, and Faerie communities whose wisdom percolates throughout these pages. Lastly, primary thanks as always to my husband, Paul, and my daughter, Lila, who hopefully won't be too embarrassed to read these stories in ten or fifteen years. In the end, now feels like the right time for these tales, which I consider the dearest to me of anything I've written, to find their way in the world, and perhaps to find a reader or two for whom they will resonate. It's a joy to share them with you now.

Jay Michaelson
July 2023

Earlier versions of the following stories have appeared before:

"The Verse," *Blithe House Quarterly*, reprinted in *Charmed Lives: Gay Spirit in Storytelling*, edited by Toby Johnson and Steve Berman.

"The Mikva of Ben Sira's Transmigration" (as "The Erotic Mikva"), *Ashé Journal*.

"The Ascent of Chana Rivka Kornfeld" (as "The Place of Anger"), *Zeek*.

"The Night Watchman and the Hundred Thousand Golems," CAJE News (winner of the Dornstein Prize in short fiction).

RABBI DR. JAY MICHAELSON is the author of nine books, including *Everything is God: The Radical Path of Nondual Judaism* and *The Heresy of Jacob Frank: From Jewish Messianism to Esoteric Myth*, winner of the 2023 National Jewish Book Award for Scholarship. He holds an MFA in Fiction from Sarah Lawrence, a PhD in Jewish Thought from Hebrew University, and a JD from Yale. Jay is a journalist at *Rolling Stone* and CNN, a rabbi, a longtime LGBTQ activist, and a teacher of Jewish and Buddhist meditation. He lives outside New York City with his husband and daughter.

AYIN PRESS is an artist-run publishing platform and production studio rooted in Jewish culture and emanating outward. We create and support work at the intersection of Political Imagination, Speculative Theology, and Radical Aesthetics.

Ayin was founded on a deep belief in the power of culture and creativity to heal, transform, and uplift the world we share and build together. We are committed to amplifying a polyphony of voices from within and beyond the Jewish world.

For more information about our current or upcoming projects and titles, reach out to us at info@ayinpress.org. To make a tax-deductible contribution to our work, visit our website at www.ayinpress.org/donate.